TO LOVE AGAIN

Since she was widowed, it has been difficult for Emma Reed and her young children, Jack and Mary. But then, Rupert Bucknall offers her a job as his housekeeper. However things do not go well. Rupert has a fearsome temper and doesn't want her or the children to remain. Since his accident Rupert has lived as a recluse, believing his scars make him hideous. But Emma, with nowhere to go, must persuade Mr Bucknall that she is indispensable.

Books by Fenella Miller
in the Linford Romance Library:

THE RETURN OF LORD RIVENHALL
A COUNTRY MOUSE
A RELUCTANT BRIDE
A DANGEROUS DECEPTION
MISTAKEN IDENTITY
LORD ATHERTON'S WARD
LADY CHARLOTTE'S SECRET
CHRISTMAS AT HARTFORD HALL
MISS SHAW & THE DOCTOR

FENELLA MILLER

TO LOVE AGAIN

Complete and Unabridged

LINFORD
Leicester

First published in Great Britain in 2011

First Linford Edition
published 2011

Copyright © 2011 by Fenella Miller

British Library CIP Data

Miller, Fenella-Jane.
    To love again. - -
    (Linford romance library)
    1. Widows- -Fiction. 2. Single mothers- -
    Fiction. 3. Housekeepers- -Fiction.
    4. Accident victims- -Fiction. 5. Love
    stories. 6. Large type books.
    I. Title II. Series
    823.9'2–dc22

    ISBN 978–1–4448–0894–0

Published by
F. A. Thorpe (Publishing)
Anstey, Leicestershire

Set by Words & Graphics Ltd.
Anstey, Leicestershire
Printed and bound in Great Britain by
T. J. International Ltd., Padstow, Cornwall

This book is printed on acid-free paper

1

Emma paused to call her son who was poking a stick into an interesting hole. 'Jack, please keep up. It would not do to be tardy on the first day of my new employment.'

She could only see his nankeen britches poking out as, for some reason, he'd stuck his head in the lush, green hedge. Her daughter, Mary, ran to extricate her little brother. The child bent down and peered through the hole. She shot backwards screaming in horror.

'Mama, there's a carriage coming. It will mow us down when it turns the corner.'

Emma dropped her precious carpet-bag in the dirt, snatched up Jack and grabbed Mary's hand. She had spied a five barred gate no more than twenty yards ahead, they would be safe from harm there. The noise of the approaching carriage filled the lane. Two huge horses were approaching at a gallop, there was no time to reach the gate. She caught a glimpse of a dark visaged man holding the reins and his coachman clutching the box beside him in desperation.

With a despairing cry she threw herself and her offspring into the hedge. The carriage thundered past and was gone around the next bend at a foolhardy pace. The birds resumed their summer song and her heart stopped hammering. Slowly she stepped out of the bushes.

'Jack, sweetheart, are you unharmed?' The little boy wriggled to be put down and, without a backward glance, ran off to fetch the stick he'd been forced to abandon. 'Mary, my love, what about you?'

'My dress is mired, and there are twigs in my boots, but otherwise I have come to no harm.' The little girl giggled. 'I think that you fared worst,

Mama. Your bonnet is over one eye and you have a bird's nest stuck to your gown.'

Emma laughed with her. However bleak the circumstances her children never failed to raise her spirits. She straightened her bonnet and removed the debris from the broken nest. 'It is fortunate, my love, that the nest was not occupied. Think of the poor fledglings!'

She returned to pick up her belongings, thanking the good Lord that the carriage wheels had not crushed her few remaining possessions. Jack, bored with his game, skipped up to her. She blinked back unwanted tears. He was so like his poor departed papa, his sunny smile, floppy brown locks and big blue eyes never failed to remind her of what she had lost at Waterloo.

Pinning on a happy smile she reached out and ruffled his hair. 'We must hurry, children. In my letter to Mr Bucknall I said we would be at Stansted Manor by noon. I do not wish to make a bad impression.'

Mary gazed up, the face so like her own, unnaturally serious for a child of scarcely ten years. 'That carriage was going too fast, Mama. Surely the driver must have known the lane was narrow here.'

'You are quite correct, my dear, but as we all survived the encounter let us say no more about it. Now, let us march like your papa, you two can lead the way and I shall follow as best I can.'

The sound of a distant church clock striking mid-day meant they would not be much past the appointed hour. Already she could see the house; she hoped the inside was less neglected then the weed infested drive. She was to be housekeeper here, she prayed it would turn out to be a safer haven than her previous position.

She shuddered as she recalled that final morning. When John had left her destitute, what remained of her savings used to pay off his gambling debts, she had immediately set about finding herself a position in a big household.

She had run her father's house efficiently for several years after the untimely death of her mother, so a housekeeping position would be ideal. She had answered an advertisement in The Times to be the under housekeeper in a substantial establishment in Hertfordshire. She would be housed in a suite of rooms on the ground floor and there had been no objection to her taking her children.

Everything had gone swimmingly for the first few weeks, then the eldest son had returned from his grand tour and everything changed. He had waylaid her at every opportunity making her life a misery. When she had, in desperation, taken her problem to her immediate superior she had thought the matter closed. However, the following day she had been dismissed without references.

With only a few pounds between herself and destitution she had scoured the newspapers until she found the advertisement for this position. The remuneration was generous, her employer had raised no objections to the children and she had thanked God for providing her with a home in the nick of time. He had even included the funds for her coach fare.

She checked her skirts were as clean as they could be in the circumstances, that her children were tidy, and walked briskly around the house to find the servants' entrance. She was obliged to pass the stables.

'Mama,' Jack tugged at her gown, 'that's the carriage that went past so fast.'

It certainly was, she would never forget the navy blue and gold paintwork that had almost taken off her nose. Her heart sunk to her boots. It could be none other than Mr Bucknall who had been driving. Had she gone from the frying pan to the fire?

★ ★ ★

Rupert glared out of his study window as the woman and her two children approached the house. She was far younger than he'd expected, and far comelier too. In her letter of application she had stated clearly that she had been married for more than a decade before being widowed last year, that she had kept house for her father for several years before that. How could this be the same person? By right she should be of middle age, not this lovely young woman who was approaching. She was above average height, of slender shape and upright bearing. It was the sight of her glorious corn coloured hair, clearly visible underneath the most hideous bonnet he'd ever set eyes on, that he could not take his eyes from.

He raised his ruined right-hand to touch the scars that marred his face, and swore. He turned, flinging his half full glass of brandy into the empty hearth. Had he not dismissed all but the most ancient of the female servants to avoid their pitying eyes? He had only appointed this Mrs Reed as house-keeper in desperation. The ancient crones that had charge of his house were ruining his health. They could cook no better than they could clean.

Foster, the butler, was only with him because he was too decrepit to find employment elsewhere. The rest had left long since. He still employed a coachman, groom and two stable hands to take care of his horses. His mouth twisted, his cattle fared better than he did. Apart from them there were two outside men who took care of the house, cows and other animals and also tended the vegetable garden.

Angrily he tugged the bell strap. It was just possible Foster would hear and come at his bidding, he needed another decanter of brandy and a fresh glass to drink it in. He would not see this woman, he would get Foster to give her a month's wages and send her packing.

★　★　★

Mary's shocked exclamation drew her attention forwards. Her eyes widened.

From the front of the house had looked intact, from the back she saw the devastation. Originally the building had been L-shaped, now the structure that had pointed west was little more than blackened beams pointing starkly into the summer sky. There had been the most dreadful fire, several years since, as now copious wildflowers and grass grew amongst the ruins. Why had Mr Bucknall not rebuilt?

First she'd discovered he drove like a madman with no regard of anyone but himself, and then this. If she had an alternative she would turn on her heel and trudge the four miles back to the nearby village. Even from the outside she could see the house had an abandoned air, the many windows grime covered, the paint peeling on the frames. From what she had learnt at the coaching inn where she had alighted earlier that day, Mr Bucknall was a wealthy man. He had made his fortune in foreign parts, had returned with a beautiful young wife and bought this huge mansion.

No one had warned her that the house had been damaged by fire, or that, for all his wealth, Mr Bucknall had let his home fall into disrepair. She recalled something that had struck her as odd at the time and was now explained. The innkeeper's wife had said no one local wished to work at Stansted Manor, that is why he had advertised in a national paper.

Her mind jerked back to the present. She must not stand here gawping when her two children were cowering in her skirts waiting for her to tell them there was nothing to fear. 'Come along, we must make ourselves known. One thing is certain, my loves, we shall have plenty to do here.'

Mary slipped a small, thin hand into hers. 'I shall help you, Mama, I can take care of Jack and do other tasks as well.'

Jack kicked his sister. 'Don't need you, I'm a big boy, I can look after myself.'

Forgetting she was supposed to be making a good impression, Mary launched herself at her brother and grabbed two handfuls of his hair. This had become a regular occurrence since they had returned from Belgium last year. Before that, they had both been of the sweetest disposition, Mary an adoring big sister and Jack the most obliging of little boys.

'Enough of that, you both promised me to behave. Do you want us to be sent packing before we have even arrived?' Her voice was harsh, she hated to speak so unkindly, but desperation drove her to behave in a way of which she was heartily ashamed.

Both children stilled and muttered their apologies. Subdued and miserable they trailed behind her to the kitchen door. She knocked and waited to be admitted. She knocked again. When no one came she decided to take matters into her own hands. She could not stand dawdling outside indefinitely, she was already a quarter of an hour past the time she should have presented herself.

The door was ajar, she stepped into total chaos. Soiled dishes were scattered on the central table, what could only have been mouse droppings amongst them. The smell of dirt and decaying food was enough to make one gag.

Jack pushed past her. 'I hate it here. It's smelly and horrible. Let's go away at once, Mama.'

'Please, don't make us stay in this dreadful place, I don't like it either. It's scary as well as smelly.'

Emma agreed with both of them. How could she take her precious children into somewhere as appalling as this? No wonder no one from the village would remain here if this was how things were. If they set off directly they might well reach the village in time to catch the evening mail coach back to London. What they would do when they reached the metropolis she had no idea, but anything must be better than this.

As she prepared to leave the kitchen door smashed open and the tallest man she had ever seen stepped in. His bulk all but filled the doorway, his unkempt black hair flew around his face and his piercing grey eyes pinned her to the floor. She recognised him as the heedless driver.

'Mrs Reed, you are late. I do not tolerate unpunctuality.' He tossed a leather bag on to the table. 'I have given you a month's wages for your trouble in coming here. You are dismissed.'

A moment before she had been determined to leave, now she was equally determined to stay. This objectionable man could not treat her and her children so casually. 'Mr Bucknall, I should have been here on time if you had not almost killed the three of us by your dangerous driving.' She tossed her head, righteous indignation fuelling her temper. 'If you think I am going to march my children back to the village you have another think coming. They are tired and hungry, as am I. I refuse to leave until tomorrow.'

His mouth snapped shut. She could almost hear him grinding his teeth. What could have possessed her to speak so forthrightly to a gentleman already incandescent with anger at her tardiness. She must apologise, it was not her place to speak out, she was constantly forgetting she was no longer a lady of means, but a member of the lower orders.

Jack emerged from his hiding place in her skirts and trotted forward to stand gazing up at the giant. 'Did you get your burns from the fire, sir? Was it very painful? I once put my hand in a flame and I cried for ages.'

Good heavens! Until that moment she had not noticed the scars that ravaged Mr Bucknall's right cheek. What she *had* seen was a powerful, angry man . . . and a very attractive one too. She ran forward to drag her inquisitive child away before he could be harmed. Too late. Mr Bucknall bent his knee and scooped the boy up.

'Has your mother not told you it is wrong to comment on another's afflictions?'

Jack reached out and ran his fingers across the scars unbothered by this abrupt question. 'I hope it doesn't hurt any more. My finger's all better. Look, I have a scar like yours.' He waved his index finger under Mr Bucknall's nose.

She held her breath, how would he react to this innocent enquiry? To her astonishment he captured the waving digit and examined it closely. 'Yes, I see it. Now, young man, if your Mama is determined to stay, you had best run along and assist her.'

He dropped the boy to the filthy flags and returned his frosty glare to her. 'I am not accustomed to being gainsaid, madam, especially by a menial. However, I find that I like your son, he has a refreshing candour. I give my permission for you to remain. But it shall be for one night, I want you gone first thing tomorrow morning.'

He nodded and vanished back into

his own domain. Emma clutched the table, her knees suddenly weak. It was Mary who said what she was thinking. 'You are a naughty little boy, Jack, that horrible man might have beaten you for your impudence. You did not think of that, now did you?'

Instead of bursting into noisy tears her son tossed his head. 'I like him, he's big and fierce and very brave, isn't he, Mama?'

She pushed herself straight and tried to gather her scattered wits. 'He's certainly the former, but what makes you think he's brave, Jack?'

'He was burnt in that fire, Mama, I bet he tried to save someone. That's why he's brave. Can we stay here for ever? I like it now.'

'Only tonight, my love. I can't think where the rest of the staff are hiding, we shall have to find ourselves a room to sleep in, and then I shall change into my work clothes and see if I can bring some order into this disgusting place.'

Rupert stormed back to the study and slammed the door behind him making the decanter and glass rattle on the desk. Foster had just been in to tell him that the remaining staff had filched whatever they could carry and departed. He was alone in this mausoleum; he wished, not for the first time, that he had perished in the fire along with his wife and baby.

Then in his mind's eye he saw the trusting face of the boy child. There had been no pity in his eyes, just curiosity. His breath all but stopped in his throat. The woman, Mrs Reed, had looked straight at him, not shocked by his appearance but furious at his rudeness.

There was only Foster and her to take care of his needs, it would be foolish indeed if he sent her packing before he could find someone to replace her. She was as little like a housekeeper as one could imagine; he frowned trying to remember what she had written in her original application. That's it, she had kept house for her father before she was married. She must be a gentle woman fallen on hard times. The last thing he wanted was a lady in the house criticising his appearance, pursing her mouth at his drinking habits, but she would do for the moment.

Tipping himself a generous measure of brandy he collapsed into the battered armchair where he spent most of his time. Stretching out his long legs he propped them on what used to be a smart side table, before his boots had ruined the surface. It was possible tonight he would get a decent repast, he'd been living on bread and cheese for months. The only reason he went into the village was to get himself a hot meal.

As he sipped his brandy his stomach rumbled loudly in anticipation of the food to come. He had quite forgot the parlous state of the kitchen and the emptiness of his pantry.

2

Emma surveyed the ruins of the kitchen. This chamber was far worse than the rest of the house, she almost felt sorry for the obnoxious man who lived here. Goodness knows what he'd been given to eat — her stomach roiled at the thought.

Tying her apron more firmly about her waist, rolling up her sleeves of her serviceable gown, she turned to her two children who were not convinced that helping to clean the kitchen was really a game they wished to take part in.

'Now, my dears, this is to be a race. The winner will be the one who can clear their section of the table the quickest.' She drew a line in the dirt at one end. 'Jack, this is your section. Mary, you do up to this line, and I'll do the rest.' She'd divided the table so that she had more than half to clear, it was her hope that they would finish simultaneously. 'Ready, go.'

Not waiting to see if her children joined in she raced to her end of the table and snatched up three filthy plates. Pivoting on one heel she pounded into the scullery to drop them into the hot soapy water she had prepared earlier. Skidding back through the door she passed her children standing open mouthed watching their mother run mad.

'I shall beat both of you if you don't get started immediately,' she cried as she dashed past.

Jack suddenly decided to join in and grabbed a plate from his end of the table, he was closer to the scullery and had already deposited his load by the time his sister arrived with hers. Mary, determined not to be outdone, threw her plate from a yard away. The cascade of water soaked all of them. Shrieking with laughter they continued to tear backwards and forwards hurling cutlery and utensils with little regard for their fragility.

It was Jack who noticed they had company. 'I say, sir, have you come to play with us? It's a capital game, and I'm winning.'

Emma, scarlet-cheeked, paused, her arms full of the last few items from her end. 'I do beg your pardon, Mr Bucknall, I'm a great believer in making unpleasant tasks into fun.' His expression was disapproving, but she was almost sure she saw his lips twitch slightly before he shook his head and retreated, leaving them to their madness.

All three of them flung their final item into the water at the same time. 'I win,' Jack and Mary screamed dancing around in excitement.

'I believe it was a tie, we are all winners. Now, who wants to wash up and who to dry?'

Leaving her offspring to wallow happily in warm, soapy water she returned to the kitchen with a pail and scrubbing brush. They should be occupied long enough for her to scrub the table. The floor had already been swept, scrubbing that would have to wait until tomorrow. She stopped dead, the water slopped on to her already soaking feet.

Good heavens! They were supposed to be leaving tomorrow, but somehow in the pandemonium she had decided to stay. In this house she would be needed, her children could play without fear of disturbing anyone, and she would never find employment that paid as well anywhere else. If it weren't for her employer being such an unpleasant man, she would feel she had landed on her feet.

By teatime the kitchen was greatly improved, not as clean as it would be in the future, but quite good enough to start preparing the evening meal. The larder was empty, but she had seen a house cow and barnyard fowl on the way in, and there must be a kitchen garden as well.

'Come along, children, we are going

on a hunting expedition. You two will need a large basket, and a basin. I shall need a basin and two jugs. We are going on a dangerous adventure, we will need to be prepared. Which of you will be the first to be ready?' There were several wicker trugs piled higgledy-piggledy in the boot room, and basins a plenty back in their correct places on the shelves.

Armed with the necessities to collect eggs, milk, cream and vegetables she led the way outside. There were not the makings for bread; the flour bin was empty and there was no fresh yeast. Tomorrow she would make a list and send the stable boy into the village to buy what she wanted. Tonight they would make do with whatever she could find.

A rheumy-eyed gardener greeted her with a gummy smile. 'Well then, madam, you come to Jethro for some nice tatties and such?'

'I have indeed. See, we have all got baskets, these are my intrepid helpers, do you think you could fill them with something nice for supper?'

With her two filthy urchins skipping along beside him, Jack, as usual chattering non-stop, the ancient gardener took them down the brick path. Every so often he stopped and pointed and they eagerly rummaged and dropped things into their baskets. Knowing they were safe she turned her attention to the chickens.

A second, equally decrepit, old man appeared from what was obviously the dairy. 'Here, missus, I've got a dozen fresh eggs for you and a jug of milk. I reckon there's a bit of butter, and some cream if you want it.'

'Thank you, that's exactly what I've come to find. I'm Mrs Reed, the new housekeeper. I shall expect fresh milk and eggs to be brought to the kitchen door first thing every morning in future.'

He doffed his cap, and beamed. 'I'm Fred, that other is me brother, Jethro. It'll be a rare treat doing for a lady again after all this time.'

In less than one half hour Emma

returned to the kitchen with Jack and Mary, all their baskets full to bursting with fresh produce. Jack was beside himself with glee.

'I'm the best hunter, Mama, I've got strawberries and beans and salad leaves.'

Mary dropped her burden on the table. 'I have freshly dug potatoes, a bunch of mint and some parsley and, four ripe peaches from the hothouse. What do you have, Mama?'

'I have eggs, milk, cream and butter. See how clever we are? We have enough here for a veritable feast.'

Whilst Mary took Jack into the scullery to wash his hands and face Emma began to prepare an evening repast for her employer. She would take the tray through to him, the dining room was in no fit state to use, and then feed herself and the children.

★   ★   ★

Rupert retreated to his study baffled by what he'd seen. He was convinced he'd

25

got a candidate for Bedlam under his roof. What in the name of Hades had been going on in the kitchen? He shrugged and resuming his usual seat, stared morosely out of the window. His eyes narrowed. What had happened to his well ordered grounds? The last time he'd looked the lawns had been well manicured, the drive weed free and the hedges clipped. Now the place was in disarray.

This had not happened overnight, it took years to achieve this air of neglect. He slumped back in his chair clutching the full glass in his hand. What was the point in keeping things as they should be when there was no longer anyone to share it with him?

When there was a sharp rap on the door he slopped his precious brandy in his lap and swore loudly. 'Come in,' he roared. It must be that mad woman come to complain there was nothing to eat.

★　★　★

Emma all but dropped the tray when she heard his barked command to enter. Straightening her shoulders she pushed open the door with her hip and walked in carrying his evening meal. Ignoring his fulminating stare, she stared pointedly at his boots which were resting on the table upon which she needed to place his tray. Slowly his feet were removed and he sat up.

'I do apologise, sir, that I have no fresh bread to accompany your meal. I shall send for provisions tomorrow. However, I hope you will be satisfied with what I've prepared.'

She deftly whipped off the napkin that had been covering the repast. 'There is an omelette, new potatoes with parsley and butter and fresh beans and salad leaves. There are strawberries and cream and baked peaches for dessert.' He was leaning forward staring at the meal. 'I'm afraid I have no idea where you keep the key to the wine cellar. I would have asked your butler, but he has mysteriously disappeared like the rest of your staff.'

'Mrs Reed, you are indeed a miracle worker. From an empty pantry you have produced a meal fit for a king. Foster will be skulking in his pantry, bang on the door and demand that he fetches me a bottle of claret.'

She curtsied neatly and whisked from the room. He hadn't disagreed with her suggestion that she send for provisions, maybe he was more sanguine about her staying now that she had proved her value by producing a delicious meal.

When she carried a similar meal into the butler's domain he stared at it wide-eyed. 'Is this for me, Mrs Reed? I'd no idea you were cooking. Has the master got the same?'

'Indeed, he has Mr Foster. He is desirous of having a bottle of claret to go with it, I should be happy to take it to him if you will tell me where I can find it.'

He dropped the cloth over his food. 'Certainly not, I shall fetch it myself. You feed your little ones, I shall take care of the master. He's not had a decent meal since the last housekeeper left six months ago.' He nodded and seemed somehow to grow taller. 'It's my task to fetch and carry for the master until we have more servants. You take care of the kitchen, Mrs Reed, leave the serving to me.'

'Mr Bucknall gave me a month's wages in lieu of notice, as I'm not intending to leave, do you think it would be in order to spend the cash on provisions and employing indoor staff?'

'An excellent notion. I cannot tell you how pleased I am that you are here, for the first time since the fire, I believe we might have turned a corner. That the master is finally able to move on.' He looked longingly at his supper getting cold on the tray. He continued as he moved into the corridor. 'Losing his wife and baby all but destroyed him, he used not to be a recluse. This was a happy house, house parties, garden parties, full of sunshine and laughter.'

Emma did not like to disabuse the

old man, her arrival had not promoted change of any sort in Mr Bucknall. All she had done was prepare them all a decent meal, she had not been employed as cook, but was quite happy to take on that role until someone else could be appointed.

Jack and Mary had devoured their supper by the time she returned to the kitchen. It was a matter of moments to make herself an omelette with the remaining eggs. 'Would you like any more potatoes? They are quite delicious, it's a long time since I've had vegetables as fresh and tasty as these.'

It was after six o'clock before dessert was finished. There had been sufficient coffee to grind and prepare a jug for her employer. Mr Foster came in carrying the tray from the study. 'Clean as a whistle. The master's eaten every scrap, and so, Mrs Reed, shall I.'

'Have you not eaten yours yet? Please, Mr Foster, eat it before it is unpalatable. I shall take the coffee through.' She smiled at her children.

'You may get down from the table, my loves. Fred said you may go and see the new calf. Do you think you can find the dairy on your own?'

They vanished before her final words were finished. Smiling she picked up the tray, checking the silver coffee pot, creamer and sugar bowl no longer looked dingy and unloved, and headed for the study. The early evening sunshine poured in through the rotunda above the central entrance hall making an intricate pattern on the black and white tiles. Unfortunately it also showed up the cobwebs, dirt and lack of polish.

She paused to gaze around. This could be a lovely house again given the proper attention. However, it would need a dozen indoor servants just to begin cleaning and several footmen would be needed to reach the lofty ceilings. Would Mr Bucknall agree to employ so many? She had found comfortable accommodation in the housekeeper's apartment, but she had yet to discover clean linen to make up the beds.

As her hand was raised to knock he called for her to enter. The door had been left ajar, her boots must have been audible on the bare boards. On entering she could not see him, he was not in the armchair as before. It was gloomy in the study, not just because the windows were filthy, but the shutters were half drawn and allowed little sunlight through.

'I have your coffee, sir, shall I put it on the side table?'

He spoke from behind her, she almost dropped the tray. 'No, give it to me, I shall have it at the desk.'

'Very well, Mr Bucknall. I do apologise for spilling the cream, but something startled me and caused me to stumble.' It was impolite to criticise one's employer, but the words were out before she could stop them.

His hands appeared and removed the tray from her grasp. It was only then she noticed he wore a black leather glove on his right hand. 'I must thank you for the meal, I did not employ you to cook but am pleased you did so. I shall not require anything further tonight.'

Her eyes were drawn to his. For a moment she was pinned by his fierce grey stare, then he looked away and she was free. He really had the most remarkable face, the scars down his right cheek hardly detracted from his looks.

In the few precious minutes she had to herself before her children came back and demanded her attention, she could not help but think about the man she was now committed to spending her foreseeable future with. Before he had been burned he must have been an Adonis, for even with the damage he was still the most handsome man she'd ever seen. He reminded her of a bird of prey, an eagle perhaps, with those piercing grey eyes.

This would not do; whether he was the ugliest man in Christendom or the most handsome, it was nothing to do with her. She was his housekeeper, a mere servant, he was so far above her in status that he would not even notice her existence. As long as he got his meals on time, his household ran like clockwork, she was certain he would not give her a second thought.

No matter that before her marriage she had been the daughter of a wealthy and respected industrialist, for her father had disowned her when she'd eloped with John. He had been a charismatic young lieutenant, irresistible to a girl who'd led a sheltered life, in his scarlet regimentals. She had been visiting an elderly aunt in Bath when she had met him at the pump room.

Within a matter of weeks she had been head over ears in love. She had reached her majority that year, so had no need to seek her father's permission, and throwing caution to the winds, she had forsaken everything she'd known to follow the drum.

She sighed. Many was the time over the years she had regretted her impulsive action, John had not proved to be a satisfactory husband. Money slipped through his fingers like quicksilver, and with two small children to take care of it had not been an easy marriage. But nothing had prepared her for the disaster that his death had brought. Penniless, and pursued by ruthless officers looking for a mistress, she had fled back to England. Since then she had barely kept the family together.

Stansted Manor would be their home now; however curmudgeonly her employer, she would not allow herself to be driven away. She would make this a happy place again, then maybe Mr Bucknall would start to take a pride in his appearance and find himself another wife. Why on earth did the idea of a second Mrs Bucknall make her heart skip a beat?

★ ★ ★

Rupert sipped his coffee, letting the dark, aromatic brew soothe his irritation. There was something about this woman that got under his skin, made him aware that he was living little better than an animal in it's filth. For the past three years he had closed himself off from the world, let his house and his health deteriorate, as he wallowed in his grief and self-pity.

This woman had turned up with her two noisy brats and turned his world on end. He was no longer a man any woman would want, wealth did not compensate for hideous deformity. It was inexplicable that a servant could somehow make him feel ashamed of his appearance, ashamed that his once beautiful home was now in disarray.

He closed his eyes and, instead of seeing flames and hearing screams, he saw a golden haired woman with sparkling blue eyes. He choked on his coffee, spluttering and coughing as he tried to get his breath. Whatever Mrs Reed was, she was not lowly born, not a true servant, but a lady fallen on hard times.

Why had he agreed to employ her? He must have been in his cups when he'd sent her the letter and included the money for her coach fare. He could not have a gentle woman under his roof looking down her nose at him, making him mend his ways. She must go in the morning. He had no wish to move on, he liked the way he lived, however reprehensible it might seem to her.

3

It was late before Emma had the kitchen ready for the morning. The children had been asleep for hours, exhausted by their long walk from the village and all the running about they'd done afterwards. The last thing Jack had said to her before he fell asleep was that he liked it here and wanted to stay for ever. Mary had not been as enthusiastic, she was a nervous girl and had not taken to Mr Bucknall. Emma was of the same mind as her sensible daughter.

She looked round the huge room; the table was clean, the smart modern range cleaned out and ready to light first thing. The extra potatoes she'd cooked were mashed with butter and cream ready to make potato pancakes for breakfast.

Her accommodation was in the basement, where a housekeeper should be; she supposed there were rooms in the attic available, but she preferred to have the children within earshot in case they woke whilst she was busy. The house was quiet, she held her candlestick high, she was certain there were both rats and mice lurking in the house. What they needed were a couple of cats to rid themselves of these vermin.

She yawned as she trudged to her rooms. She was as fatigued as the children had been, but pleasantly so; hard physical work seemed to suit her and took her mind away from what might have been if John had not perished. He had inherited a small estate in Essex, they were intending to move there when he gave up his commission. This option no longer existed for on his death the estate, and all its monies, went to a distant cousin.

Why this should be so she was not sure, had thought that Jack would inherit in his father's stead. However, when she had applied to the lawyers who were dealing with the matter she had been told in no uncertain terms that the will had clearly stated the estate should go to the next *adult* male heir and not a child.

Once she was secure in her employment, and had managed to put by sufficient funds to do so, she would employ her own legal gentleman to look into the matter. This was likely to be some time in the future, as it was still quite possible Mr Bucknall would insist that she left his employment.

When she checked the little ones they were sound asleep on either side of the large bed; she had made up the small truckle that would normally be used by a maid servant. Quietly she removed her garments and, by the flickering candlelight, sponged off as much of the accumulated dirt as she could. She had no other change of raiment suitable, fortunately she did have a clean apron and cap. The soiled ones were already washed and hanging in the scullery to dry.

Before she settled down for the

remainder of the night she pushed up the window. The room was filled with the glorious sound of nightingales singing in the nearby woods. Her spirits lifted, she leant on the windowsill and listened until her eyes began to droop. It seemed barely a moment before the dawn chorus filled the room and dragged her back to wakefulness.

Sleepily she sat up, as she did so the church clock struck five times. Excellent, the children would not rouse for a while yet, she would have plenty of time to get on with her chores before they woke. Mary was accustomed to assisting her little brother with his dressing, she was a good girl and, through necessity, old beyond her years.

She disliked putting on a gown that was not clean and pressed, but was pleased she had sufficient undergarments to remain fresh and sweet beneath. Releasing her long braid she quickly brushed it and twisted it up on to her head. She doubted it would remain in place without the added security of the cotton cap she wore to cover it.

Checking that Mary had a clean pinafore and that Jack's britches and shirt would do another day, she slipped out and walked quietly to the kitchen. She pushed open the door and found her passage blocked by a solid wall of flesh. Her startled exclamation, as liquid of some sort tipped down her pristine apron, was echoed by his rude comment.

'Sir, I beg your pardon, I did not expect to find you in my kitchen at this time of the morning.'

Mr Bucknall glared down at her. 'I was under the impression, madam, this is my house and therefore *my* kitchen. I believe I am at liberty to go wherever I please without your permission.'

She bit back an angry retort. 'Is there anything I can get for you? It will not take a moment to get the range burning, I can have your tea tray upstairs within a half an hour.'

He waved his empty pewter mug at

her. 'If you had not got in my way, I should have had cider to drink. Now the last of it is spilt. I suppose I must drink tea if that is all there is.'

Without apologising for covering her clean apron with cider he marched off muttering to himself. It was not a propitious start. She reeked like a brewery and her employer was displeased with her and it was only just after dawn.

It was a matter of minutes to strike the tinderbox and light the kindling in the range. As soon as she was sure it would stay alight she put on the kettle. Now the kitchen was a lot cleaner she could see it had been refitted with the latest appliances. The kitchen range was the height of modernity, it even had a small tap on one side from which hot water could be extracted. Of course the reservoir must be filled first, but it would make the washing of dishes, and one's person, so much easier.

The greatest innovation, in her opinion, was the fact that there was a water pump in the scullery. To be able to draw water inside the house was an unheard of luxury. Was it possible that somewhere upstairs he also had a room specially designed for bathing and one of the newfangled water closets? If she remained she would have ample time to discover these things for herself.

Mr Bucknall did not have a valet, if he had he would not be so disreputable in his appearance, she prayed this did not mean she would have to empty his commode herself. That was one job she felt herself incapable of doing.

She had used all the eggs last night, she would go out into the barnyard and forage for some more. It was a great pity there were no hams hanging in the larder, she was certain her employer would be more sanguine if he had good meat on his plate. She had counted the money in the leather bag, there was five pounds. It was a fortune to her, two quarters wages at least. For all his unpleasant habits, she could not fault his generosity.

However, she was determined to use the money to replenish the empty larder and employ at least two girls to help with the work. She hoped also to obtain the services of an indoor man who could act as both footmen and valet. Mr Foster could not do all that was required in a house this size without assistance.

Outside the air was cool and sweet, a perfect June morning. She was greeted by both Fred and Jethro. 'Good morning to both of you. I see that you are early risers too. Mr Bucknall spilt his cider.' She glanced ruefully at her wet apron. 'I don't suppose there is any out here that I could replace it with? I had not wished to upset him, I wish to stay here and make a home for myself and my children. I have not made a good impression this morning.'

Jethro touched his forelock. 'You bide there, madam, I'll fetch you a flagon. The master don't deserve it, but I'd not want you to suffer because of his bad temper.'

'I've got a dozen eggs waiting, missus, you don't need to scramble about looking. From now on me brother and I will keep you supplied with what you need.'

'I thank you. Fred, do you and your brother live at Stansted Manor?'

'That we do. Along with the outside men, we're right and tight above the stables. None of us ain't been paid since last year, but we have good pickings and live like kings. About time the master thought about his tenants, they ain't having too good a time of it.'

Emma was under the distinct impression that these old men, and the butler, thought she had come to rehabilitate Mr Bucknall. That was quite ridiculous, why should he take any more notice of her then he did of his other employees?

Mr Foster, looking more sprightly than he had yesterday, refused to let Jethro and Fred cross the threshold. 'Not in here, not in your boots. Give me the flagon, Jethro Smith. Wait there,

Fred, I shall take your items in a moment.'

'It's all right for them to come in, Mr Foster, I've not scrubbed the floor yet.'

All three elderly gentleman stared at her as if she was a ninny hammer. The butler recovered first. 'I should think not, Mrs Reed. It's not your job to do that. You are the housekeeper, a position of authority and respect. It would be quite wrong for you to scrub floors.'

Smiling at her three protectors she shook her head. 'It has to be done, Mr Foster, and as I am the only person here, it falls to me to do it.' The idea of him attempting to do this task did not bear thinking of. It was unlikely he would survive the experience.

'In which case, Mrs Reed, we must rectify that matter. Servants must be obtained from the village immediately. Under your direction this establishment will soon recover its former respectability.'

'I have funds that Mr Bucknall gave

47

me for that very purpose.' She disliked having to deceive on this point, but she had no intention of letting these three discover the money had been to encourage her to leave directly. 'I was intending to send the groom into the village this morning with a list for the local emporium.'

Jethro clicked his tongue. 'No point in asking him, he answers only to the master. I can harness the pony cart, Fred can drive you in to make the purchases yourself.'

'I cannot leave my children unattended, especially Jack, he's not yet six years of age, has not the sense to keep out of danger without supervision.' She shrugged. 'His sister is an excellent nursemaid, but he does not always mind her.'

Mr Foster exchanged glances with the other two. 'We shall supervise the young lady and gentleman, Mrs Reed. There's a piano in the drawing-room that Miss Mary can play, and Master Jack can help with the animals. They'll be perfectly safe in your absence.'

She had no option but to agree. The breakfast tray returned from the study with everything eaten, and the children were perfectly happy for her to absent herself for a few hours.

'If Mr Foster is certain I am allowed to play the piano, then my morning will be well spent, Mama.' Mary looked sternly at her little brother who was wriggling on his seat in excitement. 'You had better be on your best behaviour, Jack. If you get into trouble Mama might well lose her position and we will all have to leave here.'

'I'm a good boy, aren't I, Mama? Jethro says I can milk a cow and collect the eggs. He's going to kill a chicken for dinner. I'm going to help him do that as well.'

Emma shuddered but refrained from comment. Mary was not so tactful. 'How horrible; I think you are a nasty little boy to wish to help kill one of God's creatures.' She tossed her head and her blonde ringlets danced on her shoulders.

'If someone don't kill animals, you'd have nothing on your plate but vegetables, Miss Mary. The good Lord gave us food, it's up to us to farm it.'

Mary pursed her lips and frowned at Jethro. Emma hid her smile, the gardener had said exactly what she had been thinking. Jack scrambled down from the table and shoved his sister as he ran past. 'So there, you don't have to eat it. No chicken for Mary tonight, Mama.'

Before she could comment her son had vanished across the yard. 'You will be vigilant, won't you Jethro? I can always take him with me if you think he will be too much for you.'

'He'll do very well, missus, I'll see he gets up to no mischief. I'll have the cart round in a jiffy. Fred's gone to fetch the pony from the meadow.'

Emma needed pen and paper in order to write a list of their requirements. It would be a substantial list, not only did they need basic foodstuffs to replenish the empty larder, they also needed cleaning materials and needle and thread in order to begin mending the bed linen, tablecloths and no doubt, shirts and other items for Mr Bucknall.

Mr Foster had taken Mary to the drawing-room so she must go in search of the items herself. She had already put her cider covered apron in to soak, unfortunately her spare needed to be pressed before she could put it on and there was no time to heat up an iron on the range before she left for the village. It was not correct for her to appear without one, but she had no choice.

The library was next to the study, she must be vigilant when she passed his door, it would not do to disturb the lion in his den. She wanted to make herself indispensable, make his life so comfortable he would think twice before dismissing her.

The directions she'd been given were quite clear, the servants' stairs into the back corridor, turn right and go to the entrance hall. The library was down the widest passageway, the third door on the right. She had not needed to go back to the study since last night, Mr Foster insisted it was his place to collect and carry trays to the master. She rather thought he was protecting her, he was a lovely old gentleman, but he should be enjoying a peaceful retirement at his age.

Keeping to the shadows she slipped like a wraith through the house until she came to the chamber she sought. There was no need to knock, the room would be empty. Also the noise might alert the one person she did not wish to confront again this morning.

The door opened smoothly and she sailed in. She bruised her toes on the end of her boots she stopped so suddenly. The room was occupied, *he* was precariously perched on a small wooden ladder stretching up to remove a book from the uppermost shelf.

Seeing her, he lost his purchase and crashed backwards. This was done without the usual cursing, he fell in total silence which made the sickening thud of his head, first striking the edge of the desk, and then bouncing on the boards, far worse. For a second she was unable to move, shock and horror glued her feet to the floor. Then she rushed forward and dropped to her knees beside him.

'Mr Bucknall, I am so sorry. Can you hear me?' Blood pooled beneath his head. She had killed him. It was her fault. Snatching up her skirt she ripped off the lower half of her petticoat. Then tore this in two, quickly making a pad with one piece she raised his head and pressed the folded material against the cut. Next she wound the second strip around to hold the pad in place.

His eyes were closed, he was, she thought, deeply unconscious. She was reluctant to call out for Foster, to do so would alarm her daughter. She must wait until he came to investigate her disappearance. It could not be long before Fred came to the kitchen door demanding to know why she was tardy.

All she could do for the moment was cradle his poor head in her lap and pray that his injury was not as severe as she feared. She stared down at his blood streaked face, it was the first time she'd had the opportunity to look at him closely. Of course she had noticed the scars that puckered the right side of his face, but these were mostly hidden by his overlong black hair.

Gently she smoothed his hair away from his forehead. It grieved her to see how badly he'd been burnt; how he must have fought to save his wife and child from the blaze. Poor man — to lose a spouse was hard enough but to lose a child would be agony indeed. Her babies were her life, the reason she forgave her profligate husband time and time again. For without him she would not have her precious children.

This man was as different from her husband as chalk is to cheese. John had been blonde, slim and weak willed, not famous for his courage under fire. The man whose head she held was as dark as a raven, strong and formidable and prepared to risk his life to save those he loved. Her eyes pricked, not for her own loss, but for his. His grief must have been terrible for him to have abandoned hope like this.

His breathing was even, his colour pale but not frighteningly so. She remembered a doctor telling her you could check the pulse of a patient by putting your fingers at the juncture of the chin and the neck. Sliding her own down, she felt the roughness of his unshaven cheek beneath her fingertips. As she pressed them into the place she had been shown, his eyes opened.

4

Rupert gazed upwards through blurry eyes. His head was resting somewhere soft, a golden haired angel was staring down at him. That was a relief, he'd not been pitched into the fiery furnaces as expected. The angel looked vaguely familiar and far more anxious than an angel should.

Devil take it! It was Mrs Reed. His head was cradled in her lap. He tried to sit up but gentle hands restrained him.

'Please, sir, lie still. You have sustained a nasty injury to your head, it is going to require the attention of a physician. I am certain that Mr Foster will be here in a moment, that will be the time for you to attempt to get up.'

Her lap made a decidedly comfortable pillow, it was many years since he'd enjoyed such intimacy. He might as well make the most of it.

Emma felt his shoulders relax. Thank goodness; she was terrified that as soon as he moved the hideous gash on the back of his head would reopen and his life would be at risk. His eyes had closed, now they opened for a second time. They were fully cognizant, he knew exactly what he was about.

A strange flutter began in her chest as his mouth curved and his eyes widened. He was all but irresistible when he wasn't scowling and roaring at her. It was decidedly improper to be sitting in this manner, she was tempted to abruptly tip his head from her skirts but did not dare do so.

'My dear Mrs Reed, do you think you could explain to me how I come to be in this . . . this peculiar position? The last thing I recall I was about to remove a book from the shelf.'

Under his scrutiny her cheeks flushed. 'You overbalanced, sir, and when you fell you hit your head on the corner of the desk. I have managed to stop the bleeding temporarily, but the injury will require sutures.'

Lazily he raised his left hand and fingered the dressing she'd cobbled together. 'I see. It is fortuitous that you had about your person the wherewithal to make this bandage, is it not?'

His innocent enquiry was accompanied by a slightly raised eyebrow. Now she was puce from head to foot. The wretched man was well aware from whence they material must have come and was deliberately goading her. She refused to remain in this invidious position a moment longer.

At that precise moment Mr Foster appeared. With remarkable aplomb he nodded. 'I see, the master has met with an accident. I shall fetch Tom Coachman and the groom to assist you, sir, and send a stable boy to fetch Dr Andrews.' His words were accompanied by the distant sounds of piano music. Mary had obviously not lost her musical ability.

The butler turned and almost hurried from the room leaving her still nursing the smiling head of her employer. She glanced around the room, not a cushion in sight that she could put under him. It was insupportable to be trapped in this way, and most improper. Unwanted tears brimmed, now this gown was ruined from his gore and she had nothing else to wear apart from the one she'd travelled in yesterday.

Unexpectedly his gloved hand closed over hers. 'Don't cry, I'm not worth your tears. I know you are loathing every minute of this. Please, madam, let me lie here on my own. I do not deserve your assistance.'

'Do not say so, Mr Bucknall. I do not blame you for being irascible and for having let yourself go, what you have suffered . . . to have lost your wife and child and been injured yourself . . . no one could blame you for having lost your way.'

His harsh bark of laughter chilled her

to the marrow. 'Pray, madam, spare me your misguided and unwanted sympathy. I am as I choose to be, I find it suits me to be, as you so kindly put it, irascible and unkempt.' His elbows dug painfully into her knees and then she was free. She could not hold back her exclamation of distress.

'Mr Bucknall, I beg you do not move, already the blood is seeping through the pad I pressed on it.' Hastily she wriggled away and scrambled to her feet. Ignoring the fact that he was watching her every move she snatched up the hem of her gown and ripped another strip from her chemise.

'Hold this against the pad that is already there. Press it hard, it will stem the blood.' He didn't argue, must have sensed the urgency in her voice. With the final strip of her ruined garment she bound the second wad of material against the wound, praying it would do until the physician arrived.

When this was done she tore down the nearest curtain and folded it into a makeshift support. 'Rest on here, sir, I shall fetch a footstool for your feet. I remember now, when my husband received a similar injury, the doctor raised his feet. I've no idea why this is efficacious, but I shall do the same for you.'

The padded stool was ideal for the purpose. However his booted feet proved remarkably difficult to arrange. Each time she managed to place one to her satisfaction and turned to lift the other the first mysteriously returned to the floor. As she was on her knees with her back to the patient she had no idea if he had swooned and this was why things were so difficult.

After the second attempt she glanced over her shoulder to be met by a smile that caught her breath. He had been deliberately teasing her. 'You are impossible, have your feet any way you choose, it is no matter to me if you bleed to death.'

This time his laughter was genuine and added to her discomfiture. 'I beg your pardon. There, see, both feet neatly arranged as instructed. Please, go about your business, madam, I shall do very well here until the quack arrives. He lives but a mile from the end of the drive, he should be here in no time.'

Crossly she stared at him. His colour was better, his extraordinary eyes quite definitely twinkling. She was not going to remain in the room and be made fun of. She curtsied, but kept her head lowered not wishing to meet his eyes. 'Excuse me, sir, I must rearrange my appearance before going into the village. I am sure that Mr Foster will be back momentarily to take care of you.'

Leaving the door open she hurried out, not stopping until she was safely in her own chamber. In despair she looked at her gown, the bloodstains would never come out. She rallied, with luck the damage would be hidden by her apron. However, she could not be going to the village as she was, she must put on her travel-stained gown.

This had once been a pretty shade of blue, it was now somewhat faded from frequent washing. She had sponged it down last night, it didn't look too bad, and at least it was less like something a menial would wear. Maybe there would be sufficient money to buy herself a length of material, if the village shop stocked such items. She was an excellent seamstress and had always made her own clothes and those of her children. With the long summer days it would be possible to sew after she had finished her duties for the day, if Mary helped her with the straight seams she could have a fresh garment completed in a couple of days.

The cart was waiting outside the back door, and there was no sign of Fred or Jethro. She was quite capable of driving the vehicle herself, the pony looked amenable enough. It was of an indeterminate brown colour, with large intelligent eyes. On impulse she walked round and stroked its long nose. 'There, you are a fine young man. I'm sure we shall deal well together. Fred must be helping Mr Bucknall, so let us depart immediately. I do not wish to leave my children any longer than necessary.'

The animal snorted and blew into her hand. She scratched between his pricked ears, untethered him, and climbed nimbly on to the slatted seat. It was some time since she'd driven, but she had been quite competent in her youth at both riding and driving. Expertly releasing the brake handle, unwinding the reins from around the post, she clicked to the pony and they were away.

* * *

'Up you come, sir, we're all ready for you now.' Foster's wrinkled face loomed into view.

Rupert's vision was somewhat clouded, he was light headed; the loss of blood was taking its toll. He didn't have the energy to reply, remained slack on the carpet allowing his minions to man-handle him on to a trestle. Although he'd lost a quarter of his bodyweight since the fire, he was still a substantial burden for his men to carry.

He ought to make an effort, some-how get on his feet so they could support him, not carry him. Too late, he was hoisted up and, with the butler supporting his head, was carried with surprising ease back to a chamber. He no longer slept upstairs, only returned to his rooms in order to change his apparel occasionally. If truth were told, he no longer slept anywhere. As soon as he closed his eyes he suffered night-mares, so preferred to sit up in a chair in his study.

The men lowered him slowly, from a distance he heard someone give instructions, and then he was rolled unceremoniously into bed. He couldn't be in the study, where the devil was he? His head spun and his world went grey. He didn't fully rouse until Dr Andrews, with the help of Jethro, and the groom, hoisted him upright.

'Right, Mr Bucknall, let's see what we have here. Good grief, whoever applied this bandage most certainly saved your life.' The doctor spoke sharply to his assistant and then turned back to him. 'I shall have to shave the back of your head, you're going to need a prodigious amount of stitches. They need to go in immediately. It's going to hurt.'

It did, like the very devil. The pain brought him back to his senses as nothing else could. Why hadn't the doctor given him a decanter of brandy to dull the pain? He gritted his teeth, the nails on his good hand dug into his palm; they were all relieved when the work was done. Cold sweat bathed his forehead, he felt appalling but the quack seemed happy enough.

'There, sir, finished. I shall dress the wound, and then leave you to rest. You must drink as much as you can to replace the blood you've lost. Good red meat and claret will do the trick.'

With a few deft twists the doctor had finished, promising to return the next day to see he had not succumbed to a putrid fever, the man departed leaving him in blessed peace. This didn't last as Foster appeared at his side.

'I have watered wine, it's what the doctor suggested. He was most insistent that you drink several pints before this evening.'

Rupert took the proffered glass and downed it in one swallow, he held it out and it was refilled. He managed three before his stomach rebelled. 'Enough. Now, man, tell me where I am.' He could tell nothing from his surroundings, one bedchamber looked very like another. He was in a large bed, the sheets fresh if somewhat crumpled, but the windows overlooked a part of his grounds that he did not recognize.

Foster fussed over the pillows, he waved him away impatiently. 'You are in my chamber, sir, it was a small matter to remove myself to another room for the present. I'm afraid you were too heavy to transport upstairs, so here you are until you are well enough to move.'

Good grief! In the servants' domain — and his arrival had put the poor old fellow out of his bed. He smiled weakly. 'I thank you, Foster, I have put you all to a prodigious amount of trouble this morning. I shall not remain here for more than a night, I promise you.' The thought of being obliged to sleep and thus suffer his recurring nightmare filled him with foreboding. He would certainly vacate these rooms as soon as he was able.

Something his fair rescuer had said came back to him. 'Foster, Mrs Reed said she was going into the village. For what reason?'

'To obtain provisions, sir. Do not worry, she is not about to abandon you in your hour of need. I believe that she is God sent to this place to save us all. Already there are smiles upon the faces of the outside staff, I believe that Mrs Reed and her children . . . '

'Be silent. I want to hear no more of

this nonsense. Come back in an hour, until then leave me in peace.'

The old man retreated, apparently unbothered by his reprimand. He had heard far worse over the past three years, no doubt he too would have sloped off if he had anywhere else to go. Although he had been determined to see the back of this disturbing young woman and her brats, in the circumstances he was relieved that she had ignored his command. When he was back on his feet he would review the situation, if she could keep out of his way, then maybe he would reconsider.

His mouth watered at the thought of the delicious omelette he had eaten last night and the potato pancakes with field mushrooms she had served for breakfast. The doctor had not, as far as he knew, told him he could not eat as normal. Although he doubted he could keep anything down at the present, he was sure he would be ready for a tasty treat later on.

It was surprisingly comfortable in

this sagging bed, the morning light streamed in through the two small paned windows leaving a chequered pattern on the boards. Daytime he could sleep a little, and nightmares were much worse in the dark.

His head was sore, but no worse than he had most mornings after drinking too much. It was a luxury to be able to stretch out his limbs, to have clean linen against his flesh, he would risk going to sleep. It was three years since he'd closed his eyes for more than a few minutes at a time. Drinking to excess was the only thing that gave him respite, a drunken stupor was better than the alternative. He would never forget the screams of his wife as she called to him to save her, he'd done everything to reach her, almost perished himself in his effort, but to no avail. His only consolation was that the smoke overcame her; the doctor had told him she and the baby would have been dead long before the flames reached them.

* * *

The pony trotted eagerly down the drive but when Emma attempted to turn his head in the direction of the village he ignored her and headed in the opposite direction. Amused, rather than annoyed, by his antics she let him continue; she was intrigued to know what it was that made him so eager to travel this lane.

Within half a mile she knew the answer, the hideous sound of a donkey braying in a paddock that adjoined a row of cottages was obviously the attraction. Laughing she drew rein. 'Silly fellow, I shall let you speak to your friend but then I'm afraid we must go to the village. We shall have nothing to eat if I don't make my purchases this morning.'

To her astonishment the donkey appeared to answer. 'You'll not get him away from here in a hurry, missus, you'll need a crust to tempt him.' This speech was followed by a head appearing over the hedge. It was a young man in shirt sleeves.

'I am Mrs Reed, the new house-keeper at Stansted Manor. Are these cottages part of the estate?'

'They are. William Everett, at your service, madam. High time someone took charge up there. If you would care to wait a moment, I'll come out with a bit of bread and bribe your pony.'

This friendly exchange had attracted a small circle of spectators. None of them looked in dire straits, the children smiling, the women also. Amongst the matrons she saw at least two girls who would be ideal as maids. Had she been brought here by a higher authority to find the staff she needed? Where better than amongst Mr Bucknall's own people?

'I am looking to take on staff. I can promise things will be different there from now on. I need two kitchen maids, two parlour maids and two inside men. There will be further opportunities for employment later, I am sure.'

A ripple of excitement ran around the small group. William immediately came to stand beside her. 'I am recently back from Belgium, Mrs Reed, where I served as a manservant to an officer until he died last month from wounds he received at Waterloo. I have excellent references.'

Emma tied the reins around the post and stepped down to face the eager crowd. 'William, you are exactly the person I was hoping to find. Mr Bucknall requires a manservant, he doesn't know that is what he needs, but between us we will convince him. I need someone else who is young and fit.' She scanned the group, there was no one immediately caught her eye. Then she saw an older man, his eyes pleading, but too proud to beg.

'You, would you be prepared to do heavy work inside? I am not looking for a footman, but someone who can assist with cleaning windows and such tasks as that.'

The man stepped forward and tucked his forelock. 'I'm happy to do anything, like Billy there, I was a soldier until paid-off. Jed Jones at your service, madam.'

As William turned the cart Emma selected four women plus one Betty Turner, who was an experienced cook, so everyone told her. Two were little more than girls, they would do in the kitchen, the others were of mature years, they would be ideal as maids of all work. All of them were eager to start immediately, promised they would gather their belongings and set off within the hour.

One of the girls, Tilly, offered to accompany her to the village. 'Jenna can bring my things, Mrs Reed, we don't have much between us. If I come with you I can help you with your purchases.'

The pony, she had discovered his name was Bruno, set off at a spanking pace. He'd achieved his aim of visiting his friend and was now ready to transport them to the village in the shortest possible time. None of the people she'd taken on had asked about conditions of service or their remuneration. But then neither had she asked for more than their word as a reference. Heaven knows what Mr Bucknall would say at her temerity. Her lips twitched, the good Lord moved in mysterious ways, very likely he had caused her employer to be incapacitated for just this very reason.

Although nobody looked hungry, no doubt, like all the other country folk, they were finding times hard with corn prices being so high and the lack of employment now that so many land-owners had enclosed their fields.

With the cart laden to the brim with necessities she returned to Stansted Manor. The church clock struck midday, she had been gone for three hours. She had never left her children alone for so long. She prayed Jack had not got into mischief in her absence and that her employer never recalled how he came to injure himself.

5

Outside the Manor the eight villagers she had taken on were waiting patiently for her arrival. Jack was dancing around firing questions at the group, Mary stood talking quietly to Betty. They immediately formed in two straight lines, as if she were the mistress of the house and not a servant like themselves.

Jack hurled himself into her arms as she descended from the trap. 'Mama, have all these people come to help you? Does that mean you will not be so busy now?'

She kissed him and ruffled his hair. 'I am never too busy for you and Mary, my love. However, I am hoping I will now have time in the afternoon to resume your schoolwork. It's far too long since you and Mary spent time with your books.'

'We don't have any books, do we,

Mama? I'm glad about that, I'd much rather be playing.'

'Quiet now, Jack. I must organise these new helpers, they have been waiting for too long already.'

William, who seemed a natural leader, soon had the goods unloaded and brought into the kitchen. Betty, who must now be known as Mrs Turner although she was a spinster, took little time to discover where the items would be best placed. This left Emma to conduct the remaining women to the attics. She prayed, as she ascended the narrow wooden staircase, that the accommodation would be usable.

She emerged into a spacious landing, quite big enough to be used as a recreational area with the addition of a few sticks of furniture and some rag rugs. 'I have not had the time to come up and examine these chambers. It does not seem too bad so far.'

Tilly turned to the others. 'It's grand, madam. Better than sharing a bed with three of my sisters, I can tell you.'

'In which case I shall leave you to sort things out for yourselves. It is only three years since this house was fully staffed, there must be not only linen and bedding, but also aprons and caps, at the very least.' Emma smiled at the group and they all curtsied. 'Kindly return downstairs as soon as you are done here. I believe that male servants sleep elsewhere, I shall send William in search of those rooms later.'

Foster was waiting for her when she emerged into the passageway that connected the various rooms in the basement. 'Madam, Dr Andrews has repaired the gash in the master's head. He has given him laudanum to help him rest; I had to put it in the master's wine or he would not have taken it.'

'I have brought back a young man who is experienced as a gentleman's valet. He will take care of Mr Bucknall now. Where is the master? I take it he is not in the study.'

The old man shook his head vigorously. 'He's in my bed chamber,

Mrs Reed. I have moved upstairs for the present. We couldn't carry him up the stairs safely.'

A flicker of apprehension ran through her at the thought that this formidable gentleman was but two doors down from her bed chamber. 'That will make it far simpler to take care of him. However, I shall get the master suite cleaned and made ready. Mr Bucknall will, I am sure, not wish to remain in his study now we have sufficient staff to take care of him upstairs.'

The butler muttered to himself; she did not catch the whole of it, but was certain he was saying her employer would do as he pleased regardless of her best efforts. He shuffled off leaving her to return to the kitchen and see how matters progressed there.

★   ★   ★

At dusk Emma eventually had a few moments to herself. The children were sound asleep, the staff eating their own supper in the kitchen and Mr Bucknall also sleeping peacefully. William had volunteered to spend the night at his side but she had refused his offer. On checking for herself she had discovered her employer to have no sign of fever, no fresh blood seeping through the clean bandage around his head. He was obviously well on the way to recovery.

Her first task today had been to set the staff to cleaning the study, it had been a herculean effort, but the job was done. When Mr Bucknall returned to his lair he would find it greatly improved. The filthy drapes had been removed and replaced with clean ones found in a well-stocked linen cupboard on the first floor. The room had been scrubbed from top to bottom, the windows left wide open; he would scarcely recognize it as the place where he had wallowed in self pity these past years.

Tilly had suggested the girls cleaned the private parlour and dressing room that made up the apartment given to the housekeeper. These had been cluttered with debris, but were now fresh and smelling of beeswax. A narrow bed had been carried down from the nursery floor and put in the dressing room. Emma now had her own bed chamber, albeit a third of the size of the one she had allocated to her offspring. It had been suggested the children move into the dressing room, but she would not hear of it. Her children always came first where possible.

Mr Foster's apartment was as comprehensive as hers, William had made short work of putting that in order. The butler did not stand on ceremony, and seemed perfectly content to sleep on the male side of the house until his master was able to return to his own bed chamber. The master suite was also pristine, the bed made up, the discarded garments collected and taken to the laundry.

All in all it had been a satisfactory day. If Mr Bucknall had been *compos mentis* none of the rearrangements could have taken place. His accident had benefited everyone including himself. Mr Foster had told her the master never went to bed because he suffered terrible nightmares.

★ ★ ★

Today he had been sleeping in a bed without any signs of restlessness. It must have been lack of sleep that made him so irritable, it was possible he would be more amenable in the morning.

Mrs Turner had proved to be an excellent choice as cook. The evening meal had been quite delicious. Roast chicken with fresh vegetables from the garden followed by a strawberry tart and thick cream. She had eaten it in her parlour, the staff found it inhibiting having her amongst them.

There had been no problem of this sort at her previous employment, she and the housekeeper had eaten with the large staff. Of course, as a senior servant, she had sat at the head of the table but, apart from that, she was treated no differently from anyone else. The hierarchy below stairs was as rigid as that above. Everyone had a place and woe betide them if they did not stick to it.

With luck Mr Bucknall would remain in his bed tomorrow morning until the doctor had been. He was due to attend at 11 o'clock, so she had been told. This would give ample time to familiarise herself with the rest of the house. She had already been in the drawing-room where Mary had found pleasure in the piano, it was a grand room but one she believed Mr Bucknall would not use. When it had been cleaned to her satisfaction she would have the furniture put under holland covers.

There was a delightful room, known as the yellow drawing room, that would be ideal. The breakfast room would be used as dining room; it would be nonsensical to use the grand dining room and seat him on his own at a table that could easily accommodate more than thirty.

It remained to be seen if Mr Bucknall would acquiesce to her plans. She hoped that when he saw how pleasant the house was he would accept the changes without losing his temper. If he bellowed at any of the young girls they would turn tail. She had warned them to be as unobtrusive as possible, to do their duties early in the morning or when they knew that their master was elsewhere.

A light tap on the door roused her from her reverie. Tilly appeared. 'I've come for your tray, ma'am. Do you require anything else this evening?'

'Thank you, no, tell Cook it was delicious. Once the kitchen is cleared, if Mr Foster has no requirements, then you are all free for the rest of the evening. Tomorrow the men must clear the servants' hall so that you will have somewhere of your own to sit in your free time.'

Slowly the great house settled into silence. The small brass clock, that was her pride and joy, chimed midnight. Emma was too excited to sleep, she would go to the kitchen and make herself a hot drink. A soothing cup of milk with cinnamon and sugar would do the trick.

It was a balmy night, a full moon streamed in through the windows making a candle unnecessary. However, it was likely to be dark in the corridor so she had best take a candlestick with her. She had removed her cap and apron long ago, her feet bare beneath her skirts. She did not possess indoor slippers, her boots had to do for both inside and out and it was far cooler without them.

The nightingales were filling in the air with their song, there must be a dozen birds at least to make such a wondrous chorus. She was smiling as she glided into the kitchen and came face-to-face with Mr Bucknall.

'I did not expect to see you up, sir,

you should have rung. You should not be wondering about so soon after your accident.'

His teeth flashed white in the gloom. 'What would be the point of ringing when there is no one here to answer apart from yourself and old Foster?'

Was this the time to tell him she had appointed a manservant to take care of him? Perhaps not, she would much prefer this news to be relayed to him in the daytime when there were others in the vicinity. 'If you would care to be seated, Mr Bucknall, I will get you whatever it is you have come looking for.'

He swung out a chair with one hand and dropped into it. 'I could smell bread baking from my chamber. I should like some of that and anything else there is to go with it. I can't remember how long it is since I had bread baked in my own kitchen.'

She collected a platter on which she placed several slices of the chicken, chutney, three thick slices of bread and a generous pat of freshly churned butter. She could not understand how there could be any of the chicken left when there was so many to feed. There was also a generous wedge of strawberry tart to go with his impromptu supper.

As she carried the tray through she realised that these items had been given only to herself and her children, no one else had eaten them. Her eyes pricked, it was a long time since anyone had treated her with such kindness.

In her short absence he had been busy lighting candles and the kitchen was now bathed in a warm glow. She could not help but be aware that he had a fresh white shirt on, but no cravat and the strong column of his neck was clearly visible. She scarcely noticed the puckered skin on the right-hand side, it was part of him, nothing to be bothered by. She had seen far worse injuries in the time she had spent on the continent; most wives and loved ones were just grateful their men survived in whatever shape or form.

'Here you are, sir. I was going to make myself some hot milk, would you care for some?'

His snort of disgust made her laugh. 'Cider or coffee — either will do.'

She had noticed a fresh flagon on the cool slate shelf in the larder. All desire for hot milk had now left her, she would give him his cider and then retreat to her own room until he was done. Her bare toes curled in the thought of his reaction if he should realise how inappropriately she was attired for someone who purported to be a respectable housekeeper.

The brimming tankard was placed beside his elbow, and he nodded, his mouth too full to speak. He swallowed hastily. 'I thank you, madam, do not let me detain you. I shall douse the candles myself before I retire.'

She remembered the changes she had made to his domain. How could she prevent him from returning there tonight? The thought of the house in uproar, her children woken from their slumber, was not a prospect she relished. 'It was so kind of Mr Foster to vacate his chamber for you, Mr Bucknall. He has been obliged to remove to the attic in order to find somewhere to sleep.' Hopefully reminding him that he was not the only one in the house, that others had needs and sensitivities to be considered, might keep him where he was for tonight at least.

His eyes narrowed, becoming almost black as he digested her remark. When he spoke her confidence shrivelled. 'I am the master here, Mrs Reed, it is your place, and his, to accommodate my every wish if you care to remain in my employ. You would do well to remember it if you wish to remain here above a se'night.'

With flaming cheeks she curtsied. 'I understand exactly, sir. You have made it perfectly clear. If you require nothing else from me tonight, I will bid you good night.'

She backed out, forgetting to take her candlestick in her hurry to depart. Twice on her return to her apartment she stubbed her bare toe in the darkness. Her humiliation had turned to anger long before she scrambled into bed. The only positive aspect of the unpleasant encounter had been that he had talked of her staying for two weeks, that was a great improvement on demanding that she left in the morning.

★   ★   ★

Rupert cursed his bad temper as the lovely young woman fled from him. He had been taken aback by seeing her toes peeping from beneath her hem, a glimpse of her slender ankles had almost unmanned him making him unnecessarily harsh. Since Amy had died he had not once thought of finding himself another wife, thought himself past redemption, too damaged in body and spirit to make an acceptable husband.

But from nowhere this young widow had appeared and feelings he'd thought long gone were stirring within him. Hard times had brought her here, she was a lady born and bred, would not be working as a servant otherwise. She had been here barely two days and already he felt his world shifting beneath his feet as though he no longer had control over his own destiny. He had vowed never to love again, to do so would only lead to further grief and heartache.

Love? What maggot had got into his brain now? Mrs Reed was his employee, the fact that she had hair the colour of ripe corn and eyes as blue as the summer sky was nothing to him. He would send her on her way as soon as he was recovered. There was brandy in his study, he had intended to go there and drink it.

Something stopped him. Perhaps he would try to sleep in a bed tonight, he still felt weak as a kitten, he wasn't sure he could make his way through the house without mishap. It was nothing to do with Mrs Reed's comment about Foster, nothing at all. He was going to remain downstairs because it suited him.

Now his stomach no longer gurgled emptily, he would return to his temporary abode and pray that he did not suffer from the nightmares that plagued him whenever he was prone in bed.

★ ★ ★

Emma wasn't sure what had woken her. The hair on the back of her neck was standing up, something had frightened her awake. Was it the children? She threw back the covers and scrambled out ready to rush to their side. She was at the doorway when a cry of such despair echoed along the corridor that it almost broke her heart.

Snatching up her bed robe she dashed into the passage, it was Mr Bucknall. Her arms were barely through the sleeves when she burst into his room. He was sitting up in bed, his eyes wide open, his face twisted in agony. He was fast asleep, gripped tight by a savage nightmare.

Without a second's hesitation she ran to his side. 'Mr Bucknall, sir, wake up, I implore you. You are having a nightmare.'

His hands were icy, cold sweat trickled down his tortured face, but he did not wake. He cried out a second time and tears streamed down his cheeks. She could think of nothing else to do but what she did for her children when they were so afflicted. She climbed on to the bed beside him and gathered him close. For a moment he resisted, still moaned in that heartrending fashion, then slowly he relaxed against her. His arms somehow found their way about her waist and he pulled her down beside him.

When she tried to move away he started to toss his head and mutter. She had no option but to remain where she was, he was in danger of reopening his wound the way he was struggling.

'There, there, it's all right now. You sleep, I shall hold you whilst you rest.'

Her soothing words worked and within a few minutes of her arrival he was breathing deeply, evenly. He was fast asleep and she was beside him in bed, in her night apparel. In the moonlight she could see he was still in his shirt. That was something, she supposed. She was quite definitely inappropriately dressed, but if she remained on top of the covers until she was able to extricate herself then maybe her reputation would still be intact.

This was the second time today she had held him. His head was heavy against her chest, the warmth from his skin seeping through the two thicknesses of her clothes. As she dozed her mind drifted, when had her husband last held her in this way? Shocked, her eyes flew open. She and John had not shared an intimate moment like this since Jack had been born.

Her hand moved of its own volition to stoke his hair. Foster must have been obliged to wash it because of the blood, and now it was soft and silky beneath her touch. Somehow she slipped down the pillows until she was lying flat. As sleep claimed her she knew, like Pandora and her box, she was going to regret this escapade in the morning.

6

It was the cockerel in the stable yard that woke Emma next morning. She felt strangely warm and comfortable, believed she had not rested so well for years. It was what she had always loved best about being married to John, the closeness they sometimes found in each other's arms.

Her sleep befuddled brain cleared. John had been dead for more than a year, and they had shared nothing but arguments for the three years before that. She didn't dare to open her eyes, she recalled exactly where she was and with whom. Thank the good Lord he had now rolled away from her, perhaps she could slip away and he would be none the wiser.

With infinite care she inched her way to the edge of the bed, dropped first one barefoot, and then the other, to the boards. She froze. Had he stirred? No, his breathing was even, she was safe. After a few more agonising seconds she was on her feet and moving stealthily to the half open door. She whisked through it and ran back to her lonely bed, climbed in and pulled the sheets up to her chin.

So many strange things had been happening to her since she arrived at Stansted Manor, she was behaving out of character and yet felt more invigorated than she could remember. Perhaps living dangerously suited her better than behaving with decorum. She would make sure that Fred did not wring the neck of the cockerel, without his intervention she would be in dire straits indeed.

A gurgle of unexpected laughter bubbled forth. Why was she getting in such a pother about her reputation? She was no longer a lady but a servant, she need not give a fig for such things. As long as she behaved as would be expected of a respectable housekeeper, no one else would care one way or the other what she did in her own time. There was an unexpected freedom in her straitened circumstances that she had never considered before. She need not agonise about having spent the night in the arms of a gentleman without the benefit of clergy, both she and he knew nothing improper had taken place. That was all that mattered. Well, he, fortunately knew nothing about what had happened so that was one less thing to worry about.

She yawned, it was just after four o' clock, she did not have to rise until six — plenty of time to go back to sleep. As her eyes flickered shut; it was not John she saw smiling down at her but a black-haired, dark visaged man.

$$\star \quad \star \quad \star$$

Rupert continued to breathe as if asleep until he was certain the delectable Mrs Reed had gone. He felt wonderful, relaxed and refreshed and it was all due to the kindness of his housekeeper. He could not imagine any other woman prepared to do what she had done for him. She must never know that he had woken half an hour ago to find himself in her arms.

Somehow he had removed himself from temptation. He breathed deeply, he could still smell the faint lemon scent of her soap. Laughing he held up his own arm and sniffed, the unpleasant stench made him gag. This made her kindness even more remarkable. It was time he had a bath, pulled himself together. He had emerged from the black tunnel his life had become, suddenly had something to live for.

What was it that old fool Foster had said to him? That his blood had ruined her gown. That was something he could do for her without engendering unpleasant gossip. He stretched out, his bare feet poked out. He would return to his bed chamber today, he had had installed a newfangled bath chamber. Today he would make full use of it.

He would wait until it was light enough to see without a candle and then go up to the large box-room on the nursery floor. When he had returned from India he had brought with him many trunks of beautiful material, silks and muslins, cottons and cashmere. Amy had ignored these treasures, her wardrobe had come from the most expensive mantua maker in London. He had all but forgotten those tedious trips to Town, being obliged to rent a cripplingly expensive townhouse for the season and then dance attendance on his beloved while she dragged him to one tedious event after another.

It was he that had been overjoyed when she had become pregnant; for her it meant the end of her freedom, the loss of her figure. She had moved into the east wing after James had been born telling him in no uncertain terms that she had no wish for another child. He frowned at the memory. How could he have forgotten that they were all but estranged when the fire had killed her and his precious son?

The intolerable grief, now he was being honest with himself, was for the loss of his baby. He could scarcely remember his wife's face now. James, a beautiful child still in leading strings, was forever etched in his memory. He slammed his fist into the bedpost wincing at the pain. So that was why he was attracted to Jack . . . he had the same floppy brown hair and big blue eyes that his own son had possessed.

Perhaps it was guilt that gave him the nightmares, not because he had loved Amy too much but not loved her enough. If they had been living as man and wife neither of them would have died. Too late to repine. Today was to be the start of a new life; his excessive drinking would end, he would take control. He was quite sure his factor was robbing him blind, it was high time the man got his comeuppance and his tenants their just dues.

He flopped back on the bed, he would remain where he was until Dr Andrews visited later this morning. It was something niggling at the back of his mind, something he had observed in his perambulations last night. Good grief! Not only was the kitchen spotless, the corridor and the rooms he was using, had also been taken in hand. This was not the work of one woman and a doddery old man. Mrs Reed had taken it upon herself to appoint new members of staff. Yesterday he would have been in a black rage at her impudence, today he was glad she did not have to do the heavy work herself.

He dozed peacefully until he was roused by a smart rap on the door. Pushing himself sleepily on to his elbows he bid whoever it was come in. A smart young man in clean white shirt, smartly tied neck cloth and buff britches marched in carrying a laden tray.

'Good morning, sir, I have your breakfast here. I shall put it on the side table whilst I help you to sit up.'

Rupert was upright in seconds. 'Who the devil are you?'

'I am William Everett, at your service, Mr Bucknall. Mrs Reed has appointed me your valet. I am experienced in that position and have already taken your wardrobe in hand.'

The tray was on his lap before Rupert could protest further that he had no wish for a manservant. He scowled. The young man ignored him and continued to talk as if he was addressing an elderly invalid.

'Cook has prepared you sweet morning rolls, ham, coddled eggs and mushrooms. I have also a pot of freshly brewed coffee. Is there anything else you require?'

Faced with mouth watering food and a pot of his favourite drink it seemed churlish to continue in a bad humour. Had he not vowed to be a new man? He would start by not dismissing this William before he'd had a chance to prove his worth.

'Nothing else to eat, this will be more than adequate. However, I wish you to have a bath drawn and find me something more suitable to wear.'

'I shall return when everything is prepared for you.'

Rupert ate with relish, it would seem there was also a cook working for him. If she continued to prepare such delicious meals she could certainly stay. He would reserve judgement on his valet. The sound of childish laughter outside his door made him smile, the movement of his lips pulled on his scars reminding him that he might have recovered on the inside but his appearance was permanently damaged.

* * *

Within a few days Stansted Manor began to emerge from its dilapidated state. Emma had been delighted to discover that most of the problems were superficial, a vigorous application of vinegar and brown paper on the windows of the rooms that were in use soon had them looking as good as new. It would take more than the few people she had to effect a total change.

Mr Bucknall had not demanded to see her, not appeared in the kitchen, in fact had remained remarkably elusive. William informed her that their employer was busy overseeing the long neglected estate, had already dismissed the estate manager and appointed a local man to run things for him.

Mr Foster was rejuvenated and, as she and he were effectively in charge of the house, had taken to visiting her in her parlour during the morning to discuss what needed doing.

'It is Sunday tomorrow, I wish to attend church with my children and any members of staff who would like to come with us. Do you think it necessary to speak to him, to obtain his permission? Also, I should like to take on half a dozen more inside staff and I am sure that a further two or three footmen would be beneficial.'

'The master has never been a churchgoer, I should not bother him with such trivialities, Mrs Reed. These decisions are best left to us. On the matter of more staff, that's something I do need to discuss with him. As butler here, it is my prerogative to ask him such things.'

That was all very well in the normal run of things, but Mr Foster was absent minded, came back frequently to ask her the same questions, having forgotten what he was supposed to be doing before he had accomplished his task. 'Thank you, for your kind offer, Mr Foster, but as I am the one who has instigated the changes it behoves me to speak to Mr Bucknall. If there is to be any unpleasantness it is far better it is directed at me, than at yourself.'

'As you wish, my dear Mrs Reed. I must admit I am finding it more difficult nowadays to remember my duties.' His bushy grey eyebrows vanished under his hair. 'I do declare I have forgotten something most important. The master gave me three parcels and I had strict instructions to deliver them to you three days ago. I misremember where I put the wretched things.'

It took the combined efforts of William, Mr Foster and two parlour maids to discover the missing items. Tilly and Ann rushed in and placed the objects on a table in Emma's parlour. 'Good heavens, what have we here?' Each rectangular object was securely wrapped in calico and then string had been tied around it. She had not the heart to send the two girls away, they were agog with curiosity. 'There, I believe I have the first parcel open, I . . . ' her voice trailed away and she stared in incredulity at what Mr Bucknall had given her.

'Oh my! I've never seen the like, madam. Such beautiful material, it's the exact colour of your hair and shimmers like gold.' Tilly stretched out a tentative fingertip and stroked the fabulous silk.

'There must be some mistake. Why should Mr Bucknall give me such an extravagant gift?' Her heart was pounding, she could think of only one reason why he should wish to reward her in this way. He knew about her night-time sojourn in his bed and was, in his own clumsy way, making amends. 'However lovely the cloth, I must return it, it is of no use to me. Silk is for ladies not housekeepers.'

'Please, Mrs Reed, will you not open the other two? It would be a pity to return all if one of them would make you something new.'

Ann was quite correct. She was in desperate need of new gowns, the village shop did not stock material, it had to be ordered in especially by their customers. With quick snips of her silver scissors she undid the other bolts of cloth. The second made her gasp with happiness. 'Look at this, girls. It is perfect.' She ran the lightweight blue material through her fingers. 'It is cotton of some sort, light but strongly woven. There's more than enough here to make me two gowns and still have enough over to make Mary and Jack something as well.'

The third parcel was equally acceptable. This was by far the largest, double the weight of the other two, there must be dozens of yards rolled up here. 'This is perfect for making dresses for the rest of you. The dark grey is ideal, it will not show the marks. It is more like a cotton twill, much heavier than the other.'

She picked up the heavy parcel and handed it to Tilly. 'I hope more than one of you are expert with the needle.'

The girl nodded, her cap slid askew on her soft brown hair. 'I reckon between us we can make the gowns, ma'am. We have discovered sufficient caps and pinafores, but none of us have a change of raiment or anything smart for Sunday.'

'Then hopefully there will be enough material here to make something for everyone. I do not believe that Mrs Turner requires a new gown, she told me she has more than one already.'

How she wished that Mr Foster had given her these gifts immediately. Mr Bucknall must think her both ungrateful and impolite not to have come personally to thank him. To purchase items of this quality would cost far more than she, or her staff, could afford. However, the gold silk must be returned forthwith.

She had not seen her employer since that ill-fated night. William had informed her his master was now happily returned to his apartment upstairs. He had accepted all the changes in the house with equanimity, ate all his meals without demure in the breakfast parlour and had not seemed to notice the shrouded appearance of the main reception rooms. She had forbidden Mary to use the piano until she had asked permission, as she hadn't yet spoken to Mr Bucknall, and her daughter had been growing impatient. That was until she discovered an enormous black tomcat lurking in the undergrowth behind the barn.

It took the girl a day and a half to coax him out, and now the cat was earning his keep catching the vermin. The animal, which Mary had named Sooty, had not even objected when she'd bathed him in the copper in the laundry. Emma hoped this had removed the worst of the fleas from the animal's fur. The fact that Mr Bucknall could not abide cats was neither here nor there. Better to brave his wrath than be overrun with rats and mice.

The children were outside with Jethro, they appeared to have adopted each other, they had never had grandparents, and the old man seemed happy to fulfil that role. Indeed, the entire staff were ready to step in when needed with advice or help for Jack and Mary when she was occupied elsewhere.

Jack, who up until now had been a truthful child, insisted that he'd spent several hours in the company of Mr

Bucknall and had even been taken up in front of him when he gone out on his fierce stallion. She was sure this was a fabrication; John had never been interested in his children, had played little part in their lives, it was possible her son was beginning to see Mr Bucknall as the father he had never had. This would be a catastrophe, she must ask her employer not to encourage her son. It would make matters so much worse when eventually they moved on, as they surely would. Good things did not last forever, in her experience.

Checking her cap was straight, no errant strands of hair protruding on either side, that her apron was crisp and clean, she felt ready to go forth and find him. It had occurred to her several times that as housekeeper she should not need to wear protective covering, all menial tasks would be accomplished by those under her control. However, until she had made up a fresh gown from the pretty material she had been given, she must appear as she was.

She paused in the grand entrance hall, already it both smelt and looked far better. The magnificent oak staircase was polished, the marble tiles scrubbed clean and the tall windows on either side of the front door sparkled in the sunlight.

According to William she would find the man she sought in his study working at estate business. With the parcel tucked firmly under one arm she marched up to the door and knocked far louder than she'd intended. Immediately he bid her enter, this time he did not roar and shout.

Stepping into the room she dipped in a polite curtsy. When she raised her eyes she was astounded to see he'd stood up as if she were a lady and moved from behind his desk to greet her. Her pulse raced. Before, he had been a handsome man, now he was devastating. She could not take her eyes from him.

His hair shone with good health and was fastened, in the old-fashioned style, at the nape of his neck with a black ribbon. Even the thick white bandage did not detract form his appearance. His shirt was immaculate, his waistcoat a dazzling peacock blue, and his cravat tied in an intricate arrangement. She dared not lower her gaze to see what he was wearing *below* the waist.

7

'Mrs Reed, I had thought you were avoiding me for some reason.'

Was it her imagination or did she detect a decided glint in his eye? 'I must apologise for not coming and thanking you immediately for your generous gifts.' She could hardly tell him that his butler had forgotten to pass them on. 'They were temporarily mislaid. It was a generous gift indeed, sir, but I cannot keep this one. Material of this quality is not suited to someone of my station.'

She held the rectangle out and he was obliged to take it. She could see he was not pleased to have it given back to him in this way. Then he smiled and the breath caught in the back of her throat.

'Mrs Reed, I do beg your pardon. I should have realised that myself. Please, will you not sit down, there are various matters I need to discuss with you.'

With a slight bow in her direction he pulled out a chair and placed it on the opposite side of the desk to the one he had been sitting in. She had no option but to take it. It was highly irregular for someone in her position to sit in the presence of her employer. But then everything about this relationship was irregular.

'Mr Bucknall, no doubt you have seen the improvements I have already made in the house. However, to restore it fully I need a full complement of staff. Jack tells me you have already brought in a flock of sheep to tidy the park, and taken on sufficient outside men to bring it back to its former glory.'

He steepled his hands in front of him and nodded solemnly. Why did she think he was having fun at her expense? She could feel her irritation building, she did not care to be laughed at in this way. 'Do I have your agreement to increase the inside staff?'

'You are the housekeeper here, Mrs

Reed, you may do as you please. However I must make it very clear that I do not care for liveried footman and all that flummery. Discreet and invisible, that is what I want in all my servants.'

'Then I thank you, sir, I shall send someone to the village. I have already taken on all those available who live in the cottages nearby. Forgive me for asking, but do you have any more bolts of the darker blue material? It is perfect for the female staff, if I'm to take on more than I need to see they are dressed accordingly.'

'The trunks in the box from on the nursery floor are full of such stuff.' He tossed the parcel of gold silk back to her, his sudden gesture startled her and the item fell the floor with a thump. She had not fastened the string securely and it unrolled; yards of shimmering silk cascaded across the boards.

She exclaimed in horror at her clumsiness. This was no way to treat such delicate stuff. Scrambling from her chair she dropped to her knees and started to gather it back. Strong arms gripped her elbows and she was lifted from the floor and dropped, rather too hard, back on her feet.

'Leave it. You have girls to pick up after you, Mrs Reed. I will not have you scrabbling about the floor as if you are no better than a serving maid.' He stared down at her, his mouth firm and his expression uncompromising. 'Ring the bell. Summon a girl to pick this up. Come with me, we can continue our discussion on the terrace.' Without allowing her time to disagree he gripped her elbow and all but bundled her out of the open French doors. 'Sit there, in the shade, I shall speak to the girl when she arrives.'

He strode inside and she heard him issuing orders, no doubt they would be obeyed with alacrity. His absence gave her a precious few moments to recover her composure. She was unused to being manhandled in this way, he was a very dictatorial gentleman and she wasn't at all sure she liked him at all. He reappeared and handed her a glass of something sweet. 'Drink this, my dear, it is sherry wine, it will calm your nerves.'

Obediently she sipped and found the contents to her liking. 'I have not had this before, it is most palatable, I thank you for bringing it, sir.'

He folded himself on to the stone bench beside her. His proximity was unsettling and nervously she gulped her drink. The liquid went the wrong way and she choked. Red-faced and mortified, she was obliged to suffer the indignity of being thumped on the back, whilst gasping like a landed fish.

'I am recovered, thank you, for your assistance. I do not know why it is, but every time I am in your vicinity some accident occurs. I think we will do well to keep our meetings to a minimum in future.' She stood up and curtsied. 'I would like to ask you a favour, Mr Bucknall. Would you allow my daughter to play your piano in the drawing-room? She is a talented pianist, I can assure you it will be no hardship to listen to her.'

His gaze was no longer on her, but over her head towards the natural lake that graced the sweeping lawn. 'Is that your son, over there, by the boat shed?'

Emma followed his pointing finger. 'It is, he should not be there on his own. He is forbidden to go near water without an adult with him.'

Before she could gather her skirts and race down the slope he grabbed her arm restraining her. 'Has he been told expressly not to go down to the lake?'

Why was he delaying to ask such silly questions? 'Yes, did I not just say so? Please, sir, I must go down there before he falls in and drowns himself.'

'No, I shall fetch him back, he will come to no harm from the water. I can assure you, Mrs Reed, he will not venture there again. Go about your duties, allow me to take care of this matter for you. After all, your children are as much my responsibility as yours whilst they reside under my roof.'

Reassured by his confidence, although puzzled by his comments about responsibility, she returned to her sitting room. Mrs Turner was due to discuss the menu for tomorrow, but first she would find Mary and tell her the good news.

* * *

As Rupert jogged down to the water he wondered what had possessed him to become involved in this way. Each step jarred his head, he would be glad when the sawbones returned to remove the sutures. It was correct that anyone in his employ was his responsibility, but he wasn't sure that included the offspring of employees. However, Mrs Reed had more than enough to do running the household. And it was high time this young scamp was taken in hand. He was hopelessly spoilt, overindulged by his doting mama, in desperate need of discipline in his opinion.

The child had been told not to come near the water and had deliberately disobeyed. He doubted he would be punished by his mother, so he would administer well deserved discipline himself. A few sharp slaps on his backside would do the child no harm, and might teach him to mind his mother more. It might also save his life by keeping him away from the water.

When he was within range he raised his voice and roared. 'Jack Reed, what the devil do you think you're doing down here when you have been forbidden to do so?'

The little boy had been happily poking his stick into the water. The child, scared witless by his shout, tumbled forward and disappeared beneath the reeds. Cursing his stupidity, Rupert ripped off his jacket and waistcoat, one boot and then the other followed. He dived headfirst into the lake and swam desperately towards the bottom.

At first he could see nothing, just waving greenery and water. Then he caught a glimpse of something solid and lunged forward. His lungs were bursting. There were black spots before his eyes. He would not surface without the child. His questing fingers touched a slippery leg; he gripped it hard and shot to the surface. It was too deep to stand even for him, and the water was cold even in midsummer. The boy was limp in his arms, his head lolling to one side, no sign of life at all.

Not again, not another life lost because of him. Desperately he turned the boy over his knee and began banging him vigorously between the shoulder blades. Although a gush of water came from his mouth, Jack was still not breathing. Once, when a sailor had gone overboard, he'd watched in amazement as an Arab physician had somehow breathed life back into what had appeared to be a corpse.

Flipping the child on to his back he knelt over him trying to remember what he'd seen. Whatever he did, it could not make matters worse. Placing his own mouth over the boy's he breathed deeply, then turned his head and drew a second breath and pushed this into the boy's lungs. He turned his head away and then the miracle took place, just as it had done on the ship. The child convulsed, vomited up the remainder of the water he'd swallowed and started to weep piteously.

Scooping him up, Rupert stroked his little head. 'Hush, my brave boy, you are safe now. Perhaps you will remember not to go near the water in future.' Stopping momentarily to snatch up his jacket and wrap the shivering child in it, he ran back to the house.

When he arrived at the terrace William was waiting for him. 'Here, let me take him, sir. You must go upstairs and get yourself dry, you will have done yourself no good so soon after your accident.'

Reluctantly Rupert handed his burden over, his valet was correct. He did feel extremely unwell, he ran his hand over his dripping hair and it came away red.

At least one of the sutures had broken. 'Send for Dr Andrews, William. I fear that I shall need him as urgently as the little lad.'

★ ★ ★

'Lawks a mussy! Whatever's all that noise?' Mrs Turner jumped to her feet and bustled to the door. Emma was beside her instantly, she had hardly had time to settle behind the table for their meeting.

Tilly hurtled down the passageway. 'It's your Jack, Mrs Reed, he fell in the lake. The master got him out but he looks mighty pale. William's sent for Dr Andrews.'

The flustered girl had hardly finished speaking when William hurried round the corner carrying her beloved son wrapped in Mr Bucknall's jacket. What felt like a stone lodged in her stomach. Her voice sounded strange, as if it belonged to someone else. 'Bring him through. Mrs Turner, fetch a warming pan and hot water. Tilly you come with me.'

William waited, holding the dripping bundle, while she placed a thick comforter on top of the bed. He gently placed her child in the centre and stood back. 'Quickly, Tilly, we must strip off his wet clothes and then rub him dry with a towel. The more vigorously we rub, the quicker we will restore his circulation.'

Although he was deathly pale and cold he was definitely breathing. His eyes flickered open and he half smiled at her before slipping back into a swoon. She flung his wet clothes in a heap on the boards and dried him vigorously. Tilly rubbed one arm whilst she worked on the other. His skin was less pallid, their treatment was working.

The patter of light footsteps warned her Mary was about to arrive. 'Mama, is Jack drowned?'

'No, darling, he is cold and miserable but not drowned. Fortunately Mr

Bucknall was there to fish him out in time.'

Jack turned his head and stared at his sister. 'I told you he was brave, he's very good at saving people.'

'Dearest, raise your arms and let me slip this warm night gown over your head. Then you must get into bed and drink this hot tea Cook has sent you.'

Mary leant over and kissed her brother's forehead. 'Well, Mr Bucknall's certainly better saving people now than he was before. Mama is always telling us that *practice makes perfect*.'

'Mary, I think that is quite enough from you. Run along and make yourself useful in the kitchen. Jack needs to rest.'

Tilly smoothed the covers and stepped back with a happy smile. 'He'll do, Mrs Reed. Look, his colour's much better and his skin's warmer too. I don't reckon Dr Andrews will say any different.'

Emma looked at her son, she believed she was feeling more unwell than him at the moment. 'Jack, Tilly is going to help you with your lovely sweet tea. Mama is going to see how Mr Bucknall is after his courageous actions.'

Her apron was quite sodden, she discarded it, checked her cap was straight in the over mantel mirror and ran up the stairs to the main part of the building. It was hard to imagine what it would have been like working at Stansted Manor when the east wing had still been there. It was overlarge as it was.

William met her in the hall. 'Mrs Reed, Dr Andrews is with the master. Unfortunately Mr Bucknall has reopened his wound and it needed re-stitching. I took the liberty of sending the doctor upstairs first, word from downstairs was more encouraging.'

'You did exactly right, William. Jack is a very lucky boy and is almost fully recovered from his unpleasant experience. I should like to thank Mr Bucknall personally, would you be so kind as to let me know when it would

128

be convenient for me to come?'

'If I were you, ma'am, I should leave it for a bit. The master's a bit tetchy at the moment if you know what I mean, demanding his brandy be brought up to him.'

'Oh dear! I do hope this accident does not set him back. I shall suggest to Dr Andrews that he might forbid strong alcohol for the moment. Kindly send the doctor down when he has finished upstairs.'

The doctor declared her beloved boy to be quite well. He could get up as usual the following day. She was glad she could inform the rest of the staff that the drama was over and they could return to their duties. Her meeting with Mrs Turner was completed satisfactorily and she spent the remainder of the afternoon with one ear listening out for her son while she filled in her housekeeper's journal.

★　★　★

Jack sat up in bed and demanded his supper when he woke a second time; news from upstairs was also more encouraging. Emma left Tilly and Mary to sit with her son and sent word to William that she was on her way. Mr Foster had told her the invalid was refusing to remain in his bed, but had agreed to recline on a *chaise-longue* in the sitting room that adjoined his bed chamber.

Emma paused outside the door to steady her breathing. How did one thank one's employer for saving the life of a beloved child at the expense of his own health? Words were not adequate for what she felt, any animosity she had harboured towards him had vanished. Only Mary still had reservations, for some reason she did not take to Mr Bucknall even though he had been polite and charming in his exchanges with her.

Raising her hand she knocked quietly. William opened the door pulling a comical expression. He was obviously warning her that she was likely to get her head bitten off.

'Come in if you must, Mrs Reed, do not stand dithering in the doorway like that. William, be about your business. I've had more than enough of your fussing for one day.'

'I'm glad to see that you are fully recovered, sir, after your watery experience. I should hate to have seen you languishing.'

His sudden bark of laughter startled her. 'Touché, my dear. You are a tonic, never fail to rouse me from my ill-humour.'

It was her turn to laugh. 'Then I am thankful I had not seen you other than in the sunniest of moods, Mr Bucknall. I shudder to think how unpleasant the experience would be otherwise.'

'I suppose you must leave the door ajar, but come in and pull up a chair. Tell me how Jack does.'

She chose a footstool, the only chair was a large upholstered one which would be far too heavy for her to shift and she had no wish for him to be applied to help. Unfortunately this would mean her head was on the level with his knees. Before she could sit he grasped her forearms and neatly lifted her on to the end of his day bed.

'Sit there, I will not have you at floor level. Do not look so cross, my dear, I am merely doing you a service. I'm certain you had no wish to crouch on a stool like a child.'

Smiling ruefully she shifted to the very end of the bed making sure that not one iota of her person was in contact with him. 'Mr Bucknall, I am delighted to tell you that Jack is none the worse for his ducking. I can't tell you how distressed I am that you came to harm on his behalf. I am for ever in your debt, you are a brave and wonderful man.'

For some reason this speech did not appear to please him. He frowned and shook his head. 'He should not have fallen in, in the first place . . . '

'I will hear no more of that, sir, you

must remain a hero in my eyes.' Some perverse notion made her reach out and clasp his hands. 'Thank you, my dear sir . . . ' she got no further as he closed his fingers over hers and inexorably drew her closer.

The roughness of one hand was contrasted strangely by the smoothness of the leather glove on the other. When she was no more than an arm's reach from him he slowly raised her hands to his mouth, up turned them and kissed each palm. The touch of his mouth on her hot skin sent waves of heat racing around her body. She should protest, demand that he release her, but she was held captive by his eyes.

They darkened as she watched from grey to black. Too late she recognized the danger, was about to regain her feet, when he dropped her hands and seized her around the waist, lifted her as if she weighed no more than a feather. With infinite tenderness he settled her in his lap and with his gloved hand cupped her chin.

8

Emma was mesmerised. His hand was cool against her overheated cheek, his mouth hot on hers. It was like nothing she had ever experienced, it made what she had shared with her husband pale into insignificance. Slowly he slanted his lips across hers, pressing lightly. Then he nibbled butterfly kisses from the corner of her mouth to her ear and back again.

When his mouth reclaimed hers it was more demanding and more exciting. Heat spiralled from her toes to her crown, she was lost; adrift in an unknown place from which she did not wish to return. Then she was abruptly pushed away; losing her balance, she fell on to her knees.

Mortified by his behaviour she scrambled to her feet and spun to face him her eyes blazing. 'You cannot be civil for more than a short while before you revert to type.' Deliberately she wiped her mouth with her sleeve as if something repellent had touched it. 'That was a singularly unedifying experience, Mr Bucknall. I need not tell you that if you attempt to repeat it I shall hand in my notice immediately.'

He had turned his head away, was only then she saw fresh blood seeping through his new bandage. Had kissing her opened his wound again? Association with her family was proving to be disastrous to his well-being. 'I shall send for William to attend to your head, sir. I shall say nothing more of your reprehensible behaviour on this occasion because you saved my son's life. Consider the debt completely repaid.'

Still he did not answer. Had she disgusted him by her willing response? Did he now think her a woman of low morals and therefore contemptible? She turned on her heel and stalked to the door.

'I most humbly beg your pardon,

Mrs Reed. I took shameful advantage of you. I give you my word as a gentleman I will not importune you a second time in that way.' His voice was soft, she had to strain to hear it. 'I have no excuse apart from the fact that you are the most beautiful woman I've ever seen and I could not resist you.'

Her anger slowly seeped away. He was a man after all. Had not John told her to never be alone with any of his fellow officers for fear of what they might say or do in his absence? 'Thank you for your apology, sir, I intend to put this episode from my mind. I beg you to do the same.'

His smile was sad, he was as discomforted as herself. This time she did not curtsy, it no longer seemed appropriate after what had passed between them, instead she nodded and went downstairs to find his valet.

He was ostentatiously pacing up and down the hallway, he wished her to know he had not been eavesdropping on their private meeting. Her cheeks flushed anew; would the fact that she had been alone in her employer's bedroom be common knowledge very soon?

'William, you must attend to the master. His bandage shows sign of further bleeding.'

'Dr Andrews said this might happen, ma'am, it is nothing to be alarmed about. I hope you left him in better humour.'

It was inappropriate to discuss Mr Bucknall in this way with other members of staff. She pursed her lips and frowned. William understood, his cheeks coloured, he bowed deeply and scuttled off down the corridor to the servants' stairs.

★ ★ ★

The following day dawned bright and fair, Jack had suffered no ill effects from his near drowning, it was Mary who seemed unable to leave her little brother's side. 'Mama, it is my fault that Jack wandered off. If I had not been so engrossed in playing the piano I should have been watching him. I promise I will not let him out of my sight in future.'

Emma was relieved that Jack had not heard this pronouncement as he would have objected most volubly. 'That's kind of you, my love, but he must stay with me today at least. Then we shall see how things shall be arranged. You have a very important job, you must go round with a basket and collect the dead rats and mice that your Sooty will have accumulated around the place. I shall give you a farthing for each.'

The thought of pennies to spend was enough to send her skipping off to complete her gruesome task. Tilly, who had just arrived with the breakfast tray for both her and Jack, was more than happy to act as nursemaid whilst Emma went upstairs to speak to Mr Bucknall. She had made elaborate notes in her journal, had an excellent idea of what expenses would be needed in order to fully restore the mansion.

The house had a much more welcoming feel, with a full complement of indoor and outdoor staff it would be as grand as the house in which she had been under-housekeeper. One of the things she wished to discuss with Mr Bucknall was the appointment of a deputy for herself and Mr Foster. He was a delightful old gentleman, but decidedly absentminded and a smart young man to assist him would make the establishment run more smoothly.

The study door was open, so there was no need for her to knock: she could hear him rustling papers at his desk, all she had to do was announce herself. 'Mr Bucknall, can you spare me a few moments of your time?'

A complete stranger jumped to his feet and came round to greet her, his hand extended. 'Good morning, Mrs Reed. I am Mr Bucknall's man of affairs, Simon Tavistock. I'm afraid he has been obliged to go to Town unexpectedly and has asked me to deal with anything pertaining to the household.'

Emma shook his hand, it was a firm, dry grip, and she liked him immediately. 'I am pleased to meet you, Mr Tavistock. I have brought with me my journal, it is up to date with all the names of the female staff entered. No doubt Mr Foster has a similar document in hand.'

He grinned. 'I have done it for him, madam, I believe he finds close work difficult with his failing eyesight.' Politely he pulled out a chair and waited until she had seated herself before returning to his place behind the desk. 'I am glad that you came to see me this morning, I have a list here of things that Mr Bucknall wishes me to tell you.'

'Then please go ahead, I am eager to hear what he wishes me to know.'

'The first, and most pressing item on the agenda, is this. You are to move up to the nursery floor with your children, you will have more space there and it is more suitable for the little ones than running about below stairs.'

She nodded, smiling at him to continue. It was an eminently sensible suggestion, and would mean that she could resume some sort of school work during the afternoons.

'Mr Bucknall wishes there to be a full complement of staff both indoors and outdoors. I have already sent word to the village, and his tenants and cottagers, asking if anyone wishes to join the staff. If sufficient number do not apply then I am to place an advert in the paper.'

'That is exactly what I came to see Mr Bucknall about. I also think it's vital we have an assistant for Mr Foster and myself.'

'I can see that you and the master are of the same mind. Mr Foster will be able to remain in his own accommodation, the new man can sleep upstairs with the others. I have inspected the rooms and they are more than adequate, have fireplaces and decent furniture.'

Emma offered her journal to him for inspection. He shook his head quickly. 'There is absolutely no necessity me to see that, Mrs Reed, Mr Bucknall trusts your judgement absolutely. If you would be kind enough to enter the names of the staff in the wages book, that is all that is required. The master was most insistent that you have the afternoons free; supervising such a big household is a responsible job and he wishes you to be at your best at all times. He has also suggested that you select a maid for your personal use, she can move her belongings to one of the small box rooms on the nursery floor and be available whenever she is needed by you, or your children.'

There was no more to be said. Her only regret was that Mr Bucknall was not there to tell her this good news himself. Until she saw him again she would not know if his sudden disappearance to London was genuine, or a ruse to avoid having to see her. But he was a gentleman, he had kissed her — did this mean he would feel obliged to offer for her? She must put such foolishness away, she was a housekeeper now, not a lady.

'Thank you, Mr Tavistock, I must return to my duties. I should like all the indoor staff to be correctly dressed, I shall put as many girls as can sew, to work on making gowns. I noticed that the three indoor men are all dressed in similar fashion. Does that mean there is already a suitable supply of garments for them?'

'It does, ma'am. I must also warn you that the east wing is to be demolished. Workmen will be arriving later today, it's to be turned into a pleasure garden. It is imperative that your little ones stay away from there until the work is done.'

★ ★ ★

Five days passed before news of her employer's return from his business was given to her by Mr Tavistock. Emma could not wait to show Mr Bucknall how things had progressed in his absence. She was now the proud possessor of not one but two new gowns in the lovely blue material. Tilly was working as nursemaid and personal maid to her, a very satisfactory arrangement for all concerned. There were now a dozen new females and six footmen added to the complement, all were smartly attired.

The hideous remains of the burnt out wing had vanished as if the blackened timbers had never existed. A team of gardeners was busy clearing the remaining rubble and preparing the soil for planting. The young woman she had chosen as her deputy, Flora Duncan, had arrived from the village. She was the niece of the shopkeeper, recently widowed and eager to find suitable employment in the area. So far the arrangement was working out satisfactorily.

She and the children were in the

schoolroom when Jack, who should have been attending to his slate, tumbled from his chair and ran to the window. The schoolroom overlooked the park and the long straight drive. 'Mama, it's Mr Bucknall coming back at last. His carriage has just turned in through the gate, he will be here soon.'

Emma's heart skipped a beat. She had taken particular pains with her appearance that morning, knew she was looking her best. At three and thirty she was well past her best years, but had been told she was still a good-looking woman in spite of her advanced age. 'Jack, do not gawp out of the window like an urchin. Come and sit down immediately. You may go and play in the grounds when you have completed your letters and not before.'

He trailed back to his chair disconsolately, looking wistfully outside. She ignored him, since his brush with near tragedy she had taken heed of what Mr Bucknall had said about the lack of discipline. She would do anything to keep her children safe from harm, even if it meant being far firmer than she was accustomed to.

Within half an hour both children had finished the tasks she had set them. Jack ran to fetch Tilly who was busy with mending in the nursery. Mary watched him go with a frown. 'I hope he doesn't go down and pester Mr Bucknall, Mama. I fear he's beginning to consider him a father figure.'

Emma's elbow slipped from the table. Where had this notion come from? It was certainly not Mary's, she was but a child, someone below stairs was talking out of place. In her effort to keep Jack out of mischief she had not been taking enough notice of her daughter's needs. She had been spending far too much time listening to the gossip of the lower servants.

'What fustian, my love. It is merely hero worship because Mr Bucknall saved him from a watery grave. Come now, it is time for your practice on the pianoforte and I have several urgent matters to attend to as well.'

Tilly had taken to using the main staircase when she took the children downstairs, and now it had become the usual route. Emma knew it was not really appropriate for someone, even as important as the housekeeper, to be using these stairs, but as the days passed she was finding it more difficult to consider herself as merely a servant.

Pride came before a fall, her father had often told her. She feared this would be the case this time, that someone or something would knock her firmly from her lofty pedestal. A flash of black attracted her attention. The cat should not be in this side of the house, especially as Mr Bucknall did not care for felines. 'Mary, Sooty is loose up here. Please catch him and take him back below stairs before he is noticed.'

Her daughter skipped down the stairs and vanished down one of the many corridors calling for her pet. The double doors to the grand drawing room stood open, this was most unusual as the

147

room was not in use. She'd better close them before the cat got in there and disgraced itself.

'Ah, Mrs Reed, do come in, I have just asked for the covers to be removed. I think it is high time this lovely chamber was back in use.' He smiled, his eyes dancing with what could only be described as excitement, he held out his hand and for some reason she walked up and took it. 'I have missed you, my dear, I should not have rushed away without speaking to you first if an express had not arrived to call me to London. I will not bore you with the tedious details, suffice it to say that it was a financial matter that could not be dealt with by anyone but myself.'

Emma tingled all over from the touch of his hand on hers. She had been worrying unnecessarily, he did not think her wanton, his sudden departure had been genuine. 'I am delighted to see you, sir, it has seemed very quiet without you here.'

His rich baritone and chuckle filled

the room. He pulled her arm through his and strolled with her to a group of silk covered chairs and matching sofa. 'Please, my dear, be seated. I have something most particular to ask you.'

Her heart somersaulted, she could think of only one thing he might have to say that required her to be seated in the drawing-room. He *was* about to make her an offer, they had known each other only a short while but already she knew what her answer would be. It would be yes, not because he could offer her a life of luxury and comfort, be an excellent father to her children, but because she had fallen irrevocably in love with him. Despite his uncertain temper and disfigurement, he was the most handsome and wonderful man in the world to her.

She was relieved to sit, her legs were trembling with excitement. Her move to the schoolroom, the deference with which the staff were treating her, everything fell neatly into place. They all knew what she had failed to realise, she was to be the new mistress of Stansted Manor.

Sitting, fingers folded to stop them shaking, eyes lowered demurely, she waited expectantly. He dropped beside her on the silk upholstery. Surely this was not the way the proposal should proceed? John had gone down on one knee before her, and he was certainly not of romantical turn of mind.

'Mrs Reed, I have decided it is time that I rejoined society, and I wish you to act as my hostess. Well, what do you think of that? It will mean you must organise yourself a suitable wardrobe, I cannot have you appearing at the head of my table dressed as my housekeeper.'

Her head jerked up and she stared at him open-mouthed, not sure exactly what he meant. 'Mr Bucknall, you are suggesting that . . . that I assume the role of your wife but remain as your housekeeper.' Her hands flew to her mouth. No sooner had the words been spoken than she wished them back. *He* had not made any improper suggestions, it was *she* that had. She had not meant to imply anything of that nature, just that it was unseemly for a housekeeper to act as a gentleman's hostess.

His friendly smile changed to an expression of incredulity, then to anger. He surged to his feet. 'I am suggesting no such thing, madam, I thought you would be pleased to be given the opportunity to wear fine clothes and mix in society. We both know that you are no servant born, but a gentlewoman obliged to work for a living through no choice of her own. However, I can see that I have made a grave error of judgement, that you have misconstrued my suggestion.'

She rose gracefully, biting her lip to keep back her tears. How could she have been so stupid as to think that a man in his position would even consider taking his housekeeper to be his wife? What he had suggested was a kind offer and she had ruined the moment with her foolishness. Unable to speak coherently, she turned and fled from the room not caring any more what he thought of her rudeness.

She was still a few yards from freedom and somehow he was blocking her passage. 'My love, I have mishandled this most dreadfully. Please, do not cry, I cannot bear to see you distressed. You mean the world to me, I thought that giving you the opportunity to mix you would find yourself a husband who was worthy of you, a whole man, not someone disfigured like me.'

'I want no one else, why would you think that I needed to look elsewhere?'

He gazed down at her, his expression slowly changing from concerned to dawning hope. 'Are you telling me, my love, that you return my feelings?'

She nodded, unable to believe her dreams were to come true after all.

9

'I love you, Emma Reed, and want to marry you immediately.' He swept her up in his arms and spun round, his face transformed.

Laughing Emma threw her arms around his neck, as much for stability as anything else. 'Please, put me down. This is not the way a marriage offer should be received in polite society.' He slid her down his chest, but did not release his hold. 'Tarnation take society, I've never cared a fig for it.' His smile sent tingles of excitement all over her. 'Sweetheart, if you wish me to be conventional in this matter then so be it. I am yours to command.'

'Now that's the most outrageous untruth, sir, and you know it. However, I shall overlook your disregard for honesty and seat myself to await your offer.'

She settled back on to the sofa beginning to enjoy the role play. She was incandescent with joy; what she had felt for John had been a pale replica of the real thing. More infatuation than true love, that was why the marriage had not been a happy one for either of them.

He schooled his features and clasped his hands to his chest in dramatic fashion. 'My dear Mrs Reed, will you do me the . . . '

'Enough, this will not do at all, sir. You must be on one knee, I shall not listen otherwise.'

His expression made her giggle, with extreme reluctance he assumed the required stance. Raised a quizzical eyebrow and resumed his speech. 'Will you do me the inestimable honour of becoming my wife?'

From nowhere an imp of mischief prompted her reply. 'I thank you for your offer, Mr Bucknall. I shall give it my utmost consideration and let you know my answer by and by.'

'Saucy minx. You have already agreed, I shall hold you to that.' He sprung to his feet then resumed his place beside her, his face serious. 'I should like to be married here, in the chapel, not have banns called in church. Would you object to that?'

'I had no idea there was a private chapel at Stansted. As long as we are married in the sight of God by an ordained minister I care not where it is. However, although I have no objection to being married immediately, I do need time to gather a trousseau.'

'I believe that there's an excellent seamstress in the next village. Send for her, use the materials upstairs. I should love to see you in the gold silk.'

It was a considerable time later that all the plans were in hand. Rupert, for that is how she must address him now, insisted that she move downstairs and take a suite of rooms on the first floor. Jack and Mary could remain in the nursery with Tilly. An advertisement for a suitable governess was to be placed immediately in The Times, and the staff to be told of her forthcoming nuptials.

'And, my love, I wish to see no more of those hideous caps hiding your glorious hair.' His eyes darkened and he gathered her close. 'I cannot wait to see it loose about your shoulders, run my fingers through its silky tresses.' He lifted her until her mouth was on a level with his and then kissed her lovingly. With a sigh of regret he put her down and stepped away. 'I have deep pockets, my darling Emma. Although, as you quite rightly pointed out, I am not a biddable man, everything I have is yours. I shall not stint you or the children in any way.'

She touched his gloved hand. 'I should like to write to my father and tell him where I am and that I intend to marry again. We have been estranged too long, he does not even know he has grandchildren, perhaps this time he will be more approving of my choice.'

'Do that, I shall not go to London for the special licence until next week, then

I can combine it with the arrival of my fleet from India.'

* * *

The days sped past in a blur of happiness and excitement. Even Mary lost her reservations about Rupert, and it was a pleasure to see them interacting together. Jack, of course, was overjoyed he was to have a new papa. The seamstress proved as excellent as her reputation; she had brought with her three girls to assist in the making of gowns in fabulous colours and materials. There were to be many, Emma feared she would never have the opportunity to wear them all. Both children were also measured and new garments made for them.

The chapel, which had been disgracefully neglected these past three years, was scrubbed clean and made ready for the marriage ceremony. The rector was delighted to officiate, and appeared genuinely pleased that Rupert had found happiness after so much grief.

Rupert decided to ride to Town, William was to accompany him with the baggage horse. He was not expected to be gone more than three days, when he returned they would be married. She was as skittish as a kitten; although a mature and experienced woman, she could have been no more excited than if she was embarking on her first relationship. This is what it felt like; she had found her soul mate and believed that he had found his.

In the nursery early the following morning Jack said he had something important to ask her. 'What is it, my dear? You know you can tell me anything that's troubling you.'

'Will my new papa shout at me when I am disobedient?'

Shocked she dropped down to her knees beside him. 'Why should you ask that, Jack? Hasn't he always been kind to you?'

Tears trickled down his cheeks and

158

he shook his head. 'He shouted at me, he was so angry I fell in the lake.'

Mary overheard this comment. 'Serves you right. And anyway he fished you out again, didn't he?'

Emma's emotions were in turmoil. Had she made a dreadful error agreeing to marry a man with an uncertain temper? She must speak to him immediately, get his promise he would not treat her children roughly, not raise a hand to them in anger.

'Mary, take Jack in the garden, I shall send Tilly down to join you later.' The children left and she could hear Jack talking loudly about the accident, it would be all over the house in no time. It was imperative that she spoke to Rupert, heard what had happened from him.

She recalled how William had said his master was tetchy after the accident — this must have been the cause. A guilty conscience would have made him cross. Did she know this man well enough to spend the rest of her life with him? She had made a mistake once, rushed into something too impulsively; perhaps this was a good reason to slow things down?

Not waiting a moment longer she gathered her skirts and ran through the house, seriously startling two footmen hanging a painting in the corridor. She knocked on Rupert's sitting-room door praying he was still there, that she was in time to speak to him.

The door pushed open beneath her fingers. She was too late, he had already gone. She must speak to Tilly about this, Jack might have said more about the incident to her. Was this a good idea? Talking to the servants about such matters would surely be inappropriate? If only Rupert had told her at the time!

Undecided as to what to do next, she was hesitating on the landing when Foster puffed up the stairs waving a letter.

'This has come by express, Mrs Reed. It is addressed to yourself.'

Snapping the wax seal open she read the contents with growing dismay. 'Mr Foster, have the carriage made ready, I must leave immediately.'

Papa was on his deathbed, wished her to return to her family home at once so that they could be reconciled before he died. She could hardly refuse, it was her duty. On her return to her apartment she called for Tilly. 'Quickly, pack a trunk for the children. We must go to Essex at once. Send word downstairs for the children to come back immediately and get ready.'

The girl who acted as her abigail was efficient and soon had a trunk packed and ready to be transported downstairs. In the interim Emma wrote a quick note to Rupert explaining where she was and asking him to join her as soon as he could. She then placed it in a prominent position on the desk in his study where he would see it immediately. With a heavy heart she climbed into the carriage and sank on to the smart, navy leather squabs.

Even Jack was subdued, content to stare out of the window and enjoy the novelty of travelling in a private vehicle for the first time in his life. 'Tilly, we should be at our destination this afternoon. Cook has prepared us a delicious picnic hamper, we shall stop somewhere suitable to eat.'

As the comfortable coach trundled on she had ample opportunity to consider the implications. If her father was indeed about to meet his maker she would be obligated to go into deep mourning for at least six months. All thoughts of marriage must be put to one side until that period of time had elapsed. How could she endure the wait? At least this enforced separation had settled the doubts she might have had about the marriage. She loved and trusted Rupert, what had transpired at the lake had been an accident, she would not hold it against him.

★   ★   ★

Rupert thundered up the drive, the marriage licence and betrothal rings were burning a hole in his waistcoat pocket. He expected to be greeted by the children, Jack especially, but there was no sign of them. He vaulted from his horse and tossed the reins to William.

'Take him round to the stable, join me as soon as you may, there are things we need to put in motion for tomorrow.'

The front door opened as he reached the bottom of the marble steps. It was his man of affairs. 'Thank God you are here, sir, the house is in uproar. Mr Foster was found dead in bed this morning and neither the housekeeper nor senior footman seem capable of dealing with the matter.'

'Why does Mrs Reed not manage things?' Tavistock shuffled and looked away. 'What is it, man?'

'Mrs Reed left here three days ago, the same morning that you did. Nobody appears to know where she's gone or why she went.'

Rupert could not deal with this information now, there would be a simple explanation when he had time to discover it. He must take command of his household. 'Has Dr Andrews been sent for? What about the undertaker?'

His man of affairs had only just arrived himself and had yet to ascertain this information. Rupert examined the body, rigor mortis had already set in, the old man had been dead for some time. He was sad to see him go, but Foster had lived a decade more than his allotted time.

'As no one has thought to lay him out in his best outfit, this will have to be done tomorrow.' He turned to Tavistock who was hovering behind him. 'I shall leave this matter to you, do whatever is necessary. The funeral can be in the chapel and he can be buried in the family graveyard. I do not wish to be disturbed.'

There must be a letter waiting for him, Emma would not have left without explaining her reasons. There was nothing in the study, nothing in his apartment or hers. Taking the stairs two at a time he arrived in the nursery to find it deserted, he checked the bed chambers and the nursemaid's room, the beds had not been slept in.

The first trickle of doubt brought a sour taste into his mouth. Perhaps the old gardener would know where they had gone, Jack and Mary spent a deal of time with him. He strode through the house and round to the stable yard. William came up to him, he did not look happy.

'Mrs Reed left here in your carriage with the children and Tilly, Tom Coachman drove and Bert accompanied him, they returned without them. They went to her family home.' He fiddled with his cap. 'May I speak frankly, sir?'

'Get on with it. Whatever you have discovered I wish to know it immediately.'

'It seems that Master Jack was in the

yard and told the stable boy, who has become a particular friend of his, that Mrs Reed had been very upset to find out . . . ' he cleared his throat and ran his hand around his neck cloth as if it had grown too tight. 'Master Jack said Mrs Reed had been upset to discover you had been the cause of his accident.'

Rupert's happiness fell in ashes round his feet. He should have told Emma at the time, had known one day Jack would tell his mother whose fault it had been. She had left him, and he didn't blame her. He had all but killed her precious son and then been too much of a coward to own up. Small wonder she had changed her mind and run away.

He needed to be on his own, away from sympathetic faces, he would lock himself in his study as he used to do until he felt able to face the world again. He was sorely tempted to demand a decanter of brandy but refrained. Although his beloved had gone, she had changed him, and in her honour he would not slip back into his reprehensible ways.

Maybe she would find it in her heart to forgive him eventually, might come back one day. He would be waiting for her, she would find the house immaculate, the grounds also; all improvements he had planned to his estate, on the farms, must still go ahead. Maybe he would get in that Capability Brown fellow to landscape the gardens.

Weighed down by his grief, almost blinded by tears for what might have been, he stumbled back to his sanctuary and collapsed, head in hands, at his desk.

★   ★   ★

'Are we nearly there yet, Mama. It has been an age since you said we would be there soon.'

'Jack, my dear, can you see those tall trees through the window?' The little boy nodded. 'They are the boundary to your grandfather's estate. We shall be

167

turning into the drive at any moment. By the time Tilly has wiped your face and straightened your garments we will be there.'

Emma checked her bonnet was straight, the pretty blue ribbons neatly tied beneath her chin, that her pelisse was unwrinkled and her matching, half-kid boots unmarked. Scrambling about in a meadow with the children after the picnic could well have mired them. Satisfied she was neat, that in her new ensemble she would make a good impression on the man who valued money above family ties, she smiled at her children.

'Remember, both of you, you must be on your best behaviour at all times. Your grandfather is very poorly, that is why we are here.'

'Shall we be going home soon, Mama?' Jack asked plaintively.

Mary scowled at him. 'We cannot go back to Stansted Manor until either our grandfather recovers or he dies.' She stared earnestly at Emma. 'We will have to stay for several weeks whatever happens, won't we? I hope that our new papa will come soon to keep us company.'

'As do I, my love. I have explained it all to him in my letter, I'm sure that he will be with us by the end of the week. He was not due to return from London for at least three days, which means he should be able to join us by Saturday. I'm sure we will all be counting the hours.'

A prune faced housekeeper was waiting to greet them at the top of the well remembered steps. It had been more than twelve years since she had set foot in this house, it had never been a happy place for her, and she had vowed all those years ago not to return under any circumstances.

'Mrs Reed, the master asks that you visit him immediately. The children are to accompany you.'

Emma was allowed no time to refresh herself, to get her bearings, but was ushered directly to the rear of the house where she remembered there was a suite of rooms once used by an elderly relative. The housekeeper curtsied and held open the door.

'Come in, Emma my child, you are a sight to gladden an old man's eyes.'

To her astonishment her father, looking remarkably robust for a man about to meet his maker, greeted her warmly. She was lost for words, she had been brought here under false pretences and did not know whether to be glad her parent was not dying or angry at his deception.

Jack rushed forward and stood, hands on hips, staring at his grandfather. 'Mama was supposed to be married to our new papa, she came here instead. But you are not on your deathbed at all.'

'Hush, Jack, you must not speak . . .'

'Emma, let him alone. He is quite correct to castigate me. I beg your pardon, all of you, but I could think of nothing else that would bring you to my side. I had no idea where you were, thought you lost to me for ever. I have regretted your departure without my blessing every day since you left.'

It was only then that she realised he was unable to stand, he was sitting in an upright chair with a rug over his knees. 'I am glad that you did so, Papa, I should not have left it so long. I was young and foolish, I'm different now.' She took Mary's hand and gently urged Jack closer. 'Allow me to introduce you to your grandchildren, this is Mary and this Jack.'

Mary curtsied and Jack bowed, her father clapped his hands in delight. 'They are quite delightful, a credit to you. Now, children, I have had Cook prepare a feast for you in the breakfast parlour. I seem to remember that children are partial to sugar fancies and hot scones.' He waved at the door. 'Run along with your pretty nurse-maid, I wish to speak privately to your mama.'

Tilly, who had been waiting by the door, hurried forward and took the children's hands, the thought of cakes and other sweet treats was enough to send them off happily. Emma took the chair beside him.

He waited until they were alone and then looked shrewdly at her. 'Young Jack said something about your coming here spoiling your wedding plans. Is that true?'

'Partially so, I am but recently betrothed to Mr Bucknall, he had ridden to London to get a special licence. We were to be married on his return. I wrote him a letter explaining where I am, I am hoping he will join us here.'

'Excellent, you can be married here. I missed your first nuptials, it will be a wonderful thing to be able to witness your second. My dear girl, what a long time it has been since I saw you. Why is it that we never know how precious something is until it is lost to us?'

She reached over and took his wrinkled hand in hers. 'You were right to be angry, I behaved disgracefully and regretted my impulsiveness, the marriage was not a success. However, my union brought me the most precious things in my life so I shall never regret that it happened. Can we put the past behind us and start afresh?'

He nodded vigorously, then wiped the tears from his cheeks. 'Tell me everything that has happened to you these past years. Also, I wish to know everything about your future husband. I hope that he is a sounder choice than the first.'

'He is the most wonderful man, I cannot wait for you to meet him. I shall arrange for the carriage to return, I cannot keep his coachman and groom with me.'

★   ★   ★

The next few days were filled with laughter and happiness. She could never remember her father so jolly, he was already in the thrall of his grandchildren and was spoiling them outrageously. It was as if he was trying to make up for what he hadn't done for her.

Saturday soon arrived and she was on edge all day waiting for Rupert to appear. When he didn't she was anxious, but not unduly so. He must have been delayed in London, he would be with her very soon. A further two days and still no word. She could think of only one explanation, that he had changed his mind and wished the relationship to be at an end.

How could she have mistaken him? She had believed him to be as committed as she to their relationship. There must be another explanation, she would not entirely abandon hope until a full week had passed without word.

10

Rupert remained in his study unable to sleep, or eat and drink, until the day of Foster's funeral. It had taken longer to arrange this as the rector had been struck down by an attack of gout. He must pull himself together, his appearance at the funeral was essential. He owed it to the old man who had served him so loyally, remained at his post when all others had deserted him.

He gave the male staff permission to attend, and had ordered ale and cider to be made ready in the barn to drink the departed's health. Refreshments were also provided, he thought it a good thing to make it a celebration, rather than a time of sorrow. Tavistock was to be there in his stead; he would attend the service and committal and then return to the house.

His nightmares had returned, but this

time they were not of his wife and child but of Jack drowning in the lake. He had returned to his chair in the study, sitting there at least he could doze without fear of horrific dreams. He was lost without Emma, like one of his ship's drifting rudderless, he could not focus on the present, could not visualise a future without her and her wonderful children.

Something drew him to the butler's rooms; the young man who had taken over the position had not yet moved down from the attics. No doubt he thought it would be disrespectful to do so until after the funeral. The bed was neatly made, the room smelled fresh, one would not have known there had been a death in here a few days before.

There was still evidence of Foster's life, his faded coat hung on the back of the door. He had been buried in his new outfit, no one had yet removed his other possessions. Rupert was about to leave when something in the pocket of the jacket caught his eye. He dipped in and pulled out a letter, it was addressed to him. He recognized the handwriting, it was Emma's.

He tore it open and scanned the contents. His knees folded beneath him and he sunk on to the bed. She had not left him, her father was on his deathbed and she had gone to be at his side. She begged him to join her as soon as possible. There was no mention of Jack's accident, it was full of concern for him and how much she would miss him until he was at her side.

He leapt to his feet, rejuvenated. He could see at once how this misunderstanding had occurred, Foster had taken the letter and then died before he could pass it on. Another missive must have arrived from Essex, knowledge of this had also died with the old man.

William would be at the wake, he must fetch him. Emma would think he had deserted her, he must get to her side and put this matter right as soon as possible. The noise of the jollity could be heard as he burst out of the side door. There were so many people there, villagers, tenants as well as all his staff that it was impossible to pick out his valet.

'Mr Bucknall, are you looking for me?'

'William, good man. Mrs Reed left me a letter after all, I have just found it in Foster's coat. She was called away to visit her dying father, we must leave immediately. I should have been there yesterday.'

He would ride, but Tom must bring the carriage with his luggage. It would also be needed for when they came home. He patted his waistcoat, he knew he was grinning like a simpleton, but he cared not. He had his licence and the rings next to his heart, he would take them with him. It was just possible they might be able to marry before her father died; if they didn't, he knew Emma would insist on waiting several months until they tied the knot.

If that was what she wished, then he would acquiesce. As long as he knew that, one day, she would be his to cherish and love for the rest of her life, then he could bide his time. Tavistock appeared at the door to his study.

'Is there anything you wish me to do in your absence, Mr Bucknall?'

'Carry on as we agreed. No, there is one thing you can do. Have my chambers refurbished, they are not fit for a lady to share. Mrs Reed has already chosen the fabrics and wall coverings for her own apartment, use the same for mine.'

Tavistock looked startled but said nothing. Rupert chuckled to himself as he mounted his huge gelding, no doubt he would be the only gentleman in England with flowery bed hangings and birds and suchlike on his walls. It mattered nothing to him how his room was decorated as long as his darling girl was there to share it with him.

★ ★ ★

The weather was especially clement, Emma had arranged for meals to be served on the terrace overlooking the park. Her father had a bath chair in which his valet could wheel him around. Jack thought this an excellent game, and frequently she heard him laughing as the unfortunate manservant was obliged to push both his master and her son around the place.

She was making every effort to appear sanguine, not show her anxiety to her children or her father. He kept asking her when Rupert would arrive, she said nothing of her fear that he would never come, she had no wish to spoil the festive atmosphere. Seeing her father enjoying her company, and that of her children, meant at least that they would have a happy home to live in if Rupert did not come to claim her.

Papa retired early. The children, exhausted by a day spent picnicking outside and paddling in the shallow river that skirted the park, had also gone to bed. Emma had no appetite, was obliged to make an effort when she was with her family, but as she was on her own tonight she sent word to the kitchen that tonight she did not require dinner to be brought to her on the terrace.

It was still early, another hour or two of light before the sun set and the nightingales began their night-time chorus. She sat contemplating the vista, although the grounds were not anywhere as extensive as those of Stansted, they were very pretty. This was something she had not fully appreciated when she was living here. Her days had been over full running the household because her father had been too miserly to employ a housekeeper. There had been little time to sit and enjoy her surroundings.

The terrace was at the rear of the house, the front faced north west, the drive ran straight as an arrow to the gatehouse. At first she had spent much of her time watching this ribbon of gravel, now she was almost resigned to being abandoned and no longer watched for Rupert's arrival.

Her cheeks were wet; she was becoming a veritable watering pot lately. Would it have been better if she'd never met him? Her heart would have remained whole and she would be able to relish this reconciliation with her parent, count her blessings instead of sitting here feeling that she would never be truly happy again.

The sound of boots thudding towards her jerked her out of her reverie. She jumped to her feet, her heart pounding, her mouth dry. She was sure she recognized those footsteps. From around the side of the house her beloved appeared. It didn't matter he was several days late, he was here.

She picked up her skirts and raced towards him. 'Rupert, I have been so worried, I thought you had changed your mind.'

He opened his arms and she fell into them. He crushed her close and she tilted her face to receive his kiss. His mouth was salty, his face sweat streaked, it made no difference to the sweetness of his lips on hers. After a blissful interlude he set her down, but kept his arm around her waist.

'My darling, I thought you had abandoned me. Poor old Foster died the day I returned and never passed on your letter. I only discovered it by chance. I have been in an agony of despair without you.'

She rested her cheek against his chest and breathed deeply. Laughing, she reeled back. 'My love, I am overjoyed to see you, however do you think you could change your raiment before we continue this . . . err . . . discussion?'

'I beg your pardon, sweetheart, I have ridden pell-mell to be with you. Unfortunately I have no fresh clothes to change into until William arrives, he should not be too long behind me.'

'In which case, I shall conduct you to the apartment that has been waiting these past four days, and at least you can wash the journey from your person.'

What the staff thought of his sudden arrival she had no idea, but they rallied round and soon he was upstairs and a bath sent up to him. Suddenly her appetite returned. She was sure he must be ravenous having ridden all the way from Hertfordshire to Essex. She pulled the bell-strap in the drawing-room. When a parlour maid appeared she gave her instructions.

'Mr Bucknall has just arrived, we should both like supper served on the terrace. Ask Cook to send cold cuts, pickles and chutney, some of that delicious cheese and plenty of bread and butter.' She frowned as she thought what else they might like for their celebration meal. 'Yes, also send some of the fruit pie we had at luncheon.'

'Shall I ask Mr Thomas to send wine as well, madam?'

'Yes, and fresh lemonade if there is any. Do you know if Mr Bucknall's valet has arrived?'

The girl curtsied. 'He arrived as you rang, madam.'

Emma returned to the terrace to await the arrival of the man she loved to distraction *and* their supper. The food was already arranged on the damask covered table, candelabra lit and casting a romantic glow over the silver cutlery when Rupert returned.

'Thank the good Lord, I am half dead with hunger, my darling. I had not eaten properly for days. I believe I could devour this on my own.' He kissed her upturned mouth lightly before pulling out a chair and guiding her into it. 'Sweetheart, forgive me for saying so, but that seems a remarkably happy household for one who's master is about to depart for a better life.'

'My papa is not on his deathbed, it was a ruse to get me to come home. When he received my missive announcing my intention to marry he thought if he did not summon me immediately I might never come.'

His shout of triumph caused the

pigeons settling in the trees to leave their roosts in a flurry of protest. 'My darling, I cannot tell you how delighted I am to hear that there is to be no death in the family. I have brought the special licence with me, do you think we could be married here?'

'My father insists upon it. He can no longer walk well, but apart from that, is in good health. I am so glad I did not tell him what I feared.'

Unable to contain her happiness she left her seat and went to him. Pushing his chair back he took her on his lap, her hands moved up to rest on his cheeks. She felt the ridges of his scars, ran her fingers lovingly across them, they were part of him, she would not have him any other way.

'Rupert, my love, I cannot tell you how happy I am. A few weeks ago I was all but destitute, now look at us? I am reunited with my father and about to marry the man of my dreams.'

He encircled her waist, then deliberately removed the leather glove from his right-hand. She took it to her lips and kissed each scar. She glanced up . . . his eyes blazed.

'I love you, Emma, I do not deserve you, but I promise you I will spend the rest of my days making you and your children happy.'

'That is impossible, my darling, for I could not be any happier if I tried.'

THE END

We do hope that you have enjoyed reading this large print book.

Did you know that all of our titles are available for purchase?

We publish a wide range of high quality large print books including:
Romances, Mysteries, Classics
General Fiction
Non Fiction and Westerns

Special interest titles available in large print are:
The Little Oxford Dictionary
Music Book, Song Book
Hymn Book, Service Book

Also available from us courtesy of Oxford University Press:
Young Readers' Dictionary
(large print edition)
Young Readers' Thesaurus
(large print edition)

For further information or a free brochure, please contact us at:
Ulverscroft Large Print Books Ltd.,
The Green, Bradgate Road, Anstey,
Leicester, LE7 7FU, England.
Tel: (00 44) **0116 236 4325**
Fax: (00 44) **0116 234 0205**

TRUTH, LOVE AND LIES

Valerie Holmes

Florence Swan's plan is to escape from Benford Mill School for young women before she is forced to work in their cotton mill. Naïve, ambitious and foolhardy, she ventures out on her own, her path crossing that of Mr Luke Stainbridge — a man accused of being mad. He has returned home from imprisonment in France to discover that his home has been claimed by an imposter. Together they find the truth, disproving clever lies, and discover life anew.

BITTERSWEET DECEPTION

Liz Fielding

Kate Thornley's catering business was suffering, so she unhesitatingly accepted the offer of a contract to set up a tearoom in the grounds of a stately home. However, if she'd known that media mogul Jason Warwick was to be her boss she would have turned it down flat. His devastating good looks ensured constant female attention. Kate wasn't interested in a temporary affair — and that was all he was offering. But could she defend herself against his seductive charm?

RETURN TO BUTTERFLY ISLAND

Rikki Sharp

After thirty years' absence, China Stuart returns to her birth place, the remote island of West Uist, to attend her aunt Beatrice's funeral — and finds she has inherited Stuart Grange. As if the funeral isn't traumatic enough, James McKriven, a land developer, is claiming the rights to China's ancestral home. Amongst the cobwebs and the cracked ceilings, China finds love, but faces the ghosts of the past . . . and the reason her family fled the island all those years ago.

A COLLECTOR OF HEARTS

Sally Quilford

It's 1936. Level-headed Caroline Conrad does not believe in ghosts, but even she is shaken when strange things start happening at a Halloween House Party. At Stony Grange Abbey, the atmosphere certainly unsettles her, but the presence of the handsome, albeit changeable, Blake Laurenson increases her sense of unease. Then Caroline finds herself fighting to clear her name. She's accused of stealing the priceless Cariastan Heart — has Blake framed her? And just who is the mysterious Prince Henri?

MEMORIES OF LOVE

Margaret Mounsdon

When Emily Sinclair discovers that deckchair attendant James Bradshaw is two-timing her with Madame Zora, she sprays the details in brilliant pink paint outside the fortune-teller's caravan. It's six years before Emily sees James again and she realises that she still loves him. The only trouble is, James has purchased the Victorian play house theatre she manages and, unless she can turn its fortune around, he is threatening to close it down.

SHADOWMAN

Della Galton

Karen and Rob's show-jumping yard is in financial difficulties. And so is their marriage. Then someone starts sending nasty, anonymous letters. They seem to have an enemy who is determined to wreck their lives, but who? Is it a vindictive stranger or could it be someone closer to home ... ? Karen is determined to find out before she loses everything she loves.